"I couldn't put these books down. The drama in each story—I ate it up. I felt like I lived it, like I was really there!"

— *Dymynd F.*

"Bluford books are stories that kids and teens can relate to. Readers can use them to build courage and find solutions to their problems—instead of giving up. They are a true inspiration."

— *Michelle M.*

"I want to confess something: Before I started reading the Bluford Series, I didn't like to read at all. Now I can't stop."

— *Mariela M.*

"The Bluford Series is seriously amazing. These books made me want to read more and get off my phone."

— *Ricky M.*

"I love that these books are about the hardships young people face. They show we are resilient and can overcome anything."

— *Kennedy T.*

"Each Bluford book starts out with a bang. And then, when you turn the page, it gets even better!"

— *Alex M.*

"I found it very easy to lose myself in these books. They kept my interest from beginning to end and were always realistic. The characters are vivid, and the endings left me in eager anticipation of the next book."

— *Keziah J.*

"These are life-changing stories that make you think long after you reach the last page."

— *Eddie M.*

"My school is just like Bluford High. The characters are just like people I know. These books are *real!*"

— *Jessica K.*

"For the first time in high school, I read a book I liked. For real, the Bluford Series is *tight*."

— *Jermaine B.*

"I never liked reading until I found the Bluford Series. These books have descriptions that play like high-definition movies in my head. They are fantastic and should be read by everyone."

— *Yoriell P.*

"Each Bluford book gives you a story that could happen to anyone. The details make you feel like you are inside the books. The storylines are amazing and realistic. I loved them all."

— *Elpiclio B.*

"One of my friends told me how good the Bluford Series is. She was right. Once I started reading, I couldn't stop, not even to sleep!"

— *Bibi R.*

"I love how Bluford books take risks by addressing tough topics. They may be controversial, but they are relatable to kids going through the same things. That's one of the reasons I enjoy them. They're *real*."

— *Mia M.*

Alone

John Langan
and
Tanya Savory

Series Editor: Paul Langan

TOWNSEND PRESS
www.townsendpress.com

Books in the Bluford Series

Lost and Found
A Matter of Trust
Secrets in the Shadows
Someone to Love Me
The Bully
The Gun
Until We Meet Again
Blood Is Thicker
Brothers in Arms
Summer of Secrets
The Fallen
Shattered
Search for Safety
No Way Out
Schooled
Breaking Point
The Test
Pretty Ugly
Promises to Keep
Survivor
Girls Like Me
The Chosen
Alone

Printed in the United States of America

9 8 7 6 5 4 3 2 1

Townsend Press, Inc.
439 Kelley Drive
West Berlin, NJ 08091
permissions@townsendpress.com

ISBN: 978-1-59194-704-2

Library of Congress Control Number:
2021913381

Chapter 1

"Michael, you're not a kid anymore! You're gonna have to walk to Bluford alone. I'm too busy to go over there today."

On a hazy Friday morning, fourteen-year-old Michael Tatem stood in the kitchen, listening to his Aunt Nora list the reasons why she was skipping their appointment at Bluford High School. She was supposed to go with him for a quick meeting with the principal before he began his freshman year on Monday. But now, at the last minute, Aunt Nora had changed her mind.

"I signed what I needed to sign. If there's anything else, just bring it home," she huffed, shoving some papers toward Michael. "I'm not missing work just to hand in a bunch of forms."

"But..." Michael began and then stopped himself. He knew better than to argue with his aunt. He looked outside and felt a nervous tremble in the pit of his stomach. The school was six long blocks away, and because of his bad leg, he knew it would be a slow and painful walk. If Aunt Nora were going, she would have driven them. Now Michael was on his own.

Michael reached down and rubbed the sorest part of his leg. He couldn't remember a time when it didn't ache. He was only three when his father had gotten angry with him for drawing on a wall in their apartment. He had shoved Michael away from the wall, causing Michael to fall awkwardly against a chair. The fall broke the lower part of Michael's right leg, and because his parents couldn't afford the operation he needed, it had never healed properly.

Michael's father left him and his mother a few months later. Michael never really got to know him but had a terrible limp to remember him by.

When Michael walked, his right foot turned inward and dragged along the ground. This made it impossible to move forward without a sharp jerking movement that made his body sway clumsily. It was more than just a limp. A limp was something that people might glance at briefly, wondering if you had sprained your ankle. When Michael walked, strangers often stared. Children pointed and sometimes even laughed. Michael was almost used to it.

Stuffing the papers into his jacket, Michael walked out of the two-bedroom apartment he shared with Aunt Nora and shuffled toward Bluford High. He kept his head down with his hood pulled as far forward as possible so that he wouldn't have to make eye contact with anyone. Halfway down the block, a police cruiser approached and slowed as it neared Michael. It wasn't the first time this had happened.

"You okay?" the officer called out. He could see the officer staring at his leg. "Do you need some help?"

"No, I'm good," Michael replied nervously. "I have a bad leg, that's all."

The police officer sighed, shook his head, and drove off. Michael noticed a woman pulling her toddler closer to her and eyeing Michael suspiciously.

Ignoring them, Michael carefully stepped off the curb the instant the crosswalk sign changed to *Walk*. He knew he needed all the time the light would give him to get across the street.

More than once, he had been too slow, and the lights changed before he reached the other side. He then had to hobble awkwardly in front of people watching him from inside their cars. It felt like being trapped in a cage with everyone's eyes locked on him, as if he was a freak on display for people's amusement. Every so often, an impatient driver would honk and even yell at him.

Once when Michael was in fifth grade, a guy in a shiny black convertible had revved his engine loudly, making it seem as if he was going to run Michael over. The roaring car made him panic, and he nearly fell over. "Give me a break," Michael had muttered. The convertible sped by, and Michael noticed an ugly expression on the driver's face. The man shouted something Michael couldn't quite hear over the roar of the car's engine, but two girls sitting on the steps of a nearby apartment building turned and giggled at him. Humiliated, Michael dropped his eyes to the pavement and just kept moving. That had been years ago.

Over time, Michael had learned how to endure people staring at him. He figured out ways to hide his feelings, to turn his face into a kind of mask that seemed blank and unreachable. But that didn't mean the stares and whispers didn't bother him. Like all his classmates, Michael just wanted to fit in. But he was certain most of them didn't want him around. Who would want to hang out with someone like him?

Halfway through the crosswalk, Michael noticed three younger boys following him. He tried to keep his distance, but they approached quickly, pointing at his foot and laughing.

"Aw, man. Look at that!" shouted one of them.

"Check out his crooked foot!" added another.

"Yo, how come you walk all weird like that?" asked the tallest boy. He moved ahead of Michael but then turned and walked backward in front of him.

Michael ignored the question. He shook his head and kept moving.

"Your mama never taught you how to walk?" the tall boy asked. He stopped in front of Michael and folded his arms.

"Get outta my way," Michael said quietly.

The crosswalk sign began to blink. *Don't Walk,* it flashed.

"Look! He's like this," one of the boys behind Michael shouted. He then moved alongside Michael, imitating his limp.

"No, it's more like this!" the third boy said. He then dragged his foot in an exaggerated way, as if his whole leg were paralyzed. The boys cackled and circled around

Michael, limping and laughing in the middle of the street.

Michael focused on the crosswalk sign. If only he could get away from them. He had dealt with mean kids countless times. They usually left him alone if he ignored them, but not these kids.

Suddenly an old pickup truck screeched to a stop next to them. A dark-skinned girl with fierce, blazing eyes jumped out. She was big, but she moved quickly, her strong arms slamming the truck door shut with an angry bang. She marched up to the boys and waved a finger at them.

"You ain't got nothing better to do?" she yelled over the noise of the traffic. "Y'all think you're being funny? 'Cause this ain't funny."

The two smaller boys stepped back, but the tall one shrugged as if he were unimpressed.

"Is this how your mama taught you to treat people?" she fumed, inching closer to him. "How would you like it if somebody did this to you?"

Michael managed to reach the other side of the street but turned to watch. The tall boy stood near the curb looking sullenly at the girl.

"I don't care," he grumbled, crossing his arms.

"You better start caring!" she fumed, glaring at the retreating boys. "The little kids at my daycare center show more respect than you. They got more sense, too. You best go home with your little friends until you figure out how to treat people right."

"I don't take no orders from girls," the tall boy snapped. "Especially not from fat girls," he added. He spit his gum at the girl and called her a foul name.

"*Excuse* me?"

Just then the driver-side door of the truck opened, and a muscular teenage boy in a navy hoodie emerged. The words *Bluford Football* glowed in bright yellow letters on his chest, and his head was shaved completely bald. Michael could see he had a kind face, but his eyes were strong and intense.

"Is there a problem?" he asked calmly, stepping up to the kid while resting his hand on the girl's shoulder.

The tall boy looked away. Then he scratched his head nervously and mumbled, "Ain't no problem."

"That's what I thought." The muscular teen glanced at Michael and gave him a friendly nod before turning back to the tall boy. "Go on home, bro," he said. "You're not impressing anyone by making fun of people and spitting gum at a girl."

The kid looked away but rolled his eyes. "Man, whatever," he groaned.

"*Whatever*?" the teen repeated in a booming voice. "You want to say that again?"

The younger boy backed away slowly. Then he turned around and headed off down the street, glancing back several times. Finally, he took off running. He sprinted so wildly that he nearly lost his balance. When he was half a block away, he turned and screamed as loudly as he could, "Ain't scared of you. AT ALL!"

The muscular teen took a lunging step as if he was going to chase the kid but then stopped short with a grin. The tall boy took off like a flash around a corner.

Michael was relieved but also embarrassed that someone had to come to his rescue. "Thanks," Michael said shyly. "Sorry y'all had to get out of your car and everything."

"Ain't no big thing," the girl said. "I can't stand it when kids bully and start trouble over nothing. No reason to act that way. Know what I mean?"

Michael nodded. He wished everyone felt that way, though he didn't say it. An awkward silence spread over them. He wondered if he should say goodbye to the two strangers. After all, they probably had someplace to go and maybe friends to meet.

"You go to Bluford?" the girl finally asked.

"Yeah. I'm starting Monday as a freshman," Michael answered. "Going there right now to drop off some forms and stuff."

"Oh, I remember all about being a freshman," the girl said. "The first year is the hardest, but things get better. You'll see. There's good people there."

The older boy nodded in agreement. Then he gave the girl a sly look and said, "I know you don't remember *everything* about freshman year. Like ignoring me and thinking you were *all that* with that hairdo you had. Girl, that was more like a hair *don't*!"

"I was *all that* back then," the girl boomed, trying to keep a straight face. "And I still am," she added, poking the boy in the ribs until they both laughed.

Michael smiled. He wished he could be friends with them, but they were older—probably juniors or seniors. They had it all figured out, and Michael felt as though he knew nothing at all.

"Well, good luck to you," the girl said to Michael. "I'm Tarah, by the way, and this is Cooper."

"I'm Michael," he replied, still feeling embarrassed that he had needed their help to chase away three little kids.

Cooper reached out and shook Michael's hand firmly. "Take care of yourself, Michael. You need anything, find us. You'll see us around."

"Sure. Thanks," Michael mumbled. He saw Tarah glance over at their truck and then back at him. She looked as though she wanted to say something, and Michael wondered if she was thinking of offering him a ride. But the school was only a few blocks away. And Michael knew Tarah didn't want to show that she felt sorry for him—he could see it in her face.

"See you at Bluford!" she said instead, as she and Cooper walked back to the truck.

Watching them drive away, Michael thought of the only time he had ever ridden in a truck. It had been with an elderly neighbor, Mr. Sutton, who had lived down the hall in Michael's old apartment building—back when Michael was six years old. Mr. Sutton had let him sit up front one afternoon when the two of them went out for ice cream.

As Michael resumed the slow walk to Bluford, he thought of his life back then. It was just before he had started first grade. In some ways, Michael had felt the same way about starting school then as he did now: nervous and unsure. But in many other ways, Michael had been a completely different person.

It was before he had understood the pain of loss. It was a time before he had experienced just how cruel people could be.

It was a time before he had come to feel so completely alone.

Chapter 2

Michael was six years old the day his life changed forever. He was living with his mother in their small apartment and being cared for by Mrs. Sutton, their neighbor, while Mom was at work. He remembered it all as if it was yesterday.

"Your mother will be here any minute now," Mrs. Sutton had said with the warm smile she always gave him. "I'll bet I can sneak you just one more cookie before she gets here."

"Yum!" Michael cheered as he busily colored a dinosaur in his new coloring book. Just days earlier, he had lost a tooth and Mom had him put it under his pillow, promising that the Tooth Fairy would leave him a gift. Michael had trouble believing there was a magic fairy who would sneak into his room, but he listened to Mom.

The next morning, he found a brand-new coloring book peeking out from under his pillow. He told Mrs. Sutton all about it.

"Well, I got five dollars when I lost my tooth," bragged Nikki, a kindergartner Mrs. Sutton also watched after school. Nikki was missing two of her front teeth and Michael thought she looked like a Halloween jack-o'-lantern. "Your mama must be poor," Nikki teased.

"She is not!" Michael shouted. He didn't really understand what being poor meant, but he didn't want Nikki saying anything bad about his mom. So what if she got five dollars? Mom gave Michael the *best* things. Sometimes it was a new book from the library, filled with pictures of dinosaurs. Sometimes it was a funny song that she had made up. And sometimes, best of all, it was a big hug.

"You know what the best thing in the world is?" Mom would ask as she squeezed Michael in her arms at the end of the day. "As long as I have you and you have me, we'll never be alone. What could be better than that?"

Michael had almost finished coloring the horns on his triceratops when he heard a familiar knock on Mrs. Sutton's door.

"Mama!" Michael shouted. He wished he could sprint across the room the way Nikki did when her father came to pick her up. Instead, he shuffled in his slow, awkward way, unable to jump or run at all.

"You move funny," Nikki giggled. She pointed at Michael's foot as he limped toward his mom.

"Now, I told you before to stop that," Mrs. Sutton said sharply to Nikki. "It's not nice."

Michael ignored them and threw his arms around Mom. When she leaned over to kiss the top of his head, Michael saw her face and knew something wasn't right. Her skin seemed washed out and gray, and her expression was almost crooked.

"You feeling okay, Donna?" Mrs. Sutton asked. "You look like you've had a rough day."

Mom slowly ran her hand over her face and shook her head. "I just feel worn out. I'm sure it's nothing a little extra sleep tonight won't take care of. Just gotta get dinner fixed first."

Mrs. Sutton gazed at Mom and then said, "You hold on just a second." She hurried into her small kitchen and rattled around, banging a few pots and pans.

Then she reappeared with a covered dish in her hands.

"What's this?"

"Dinner. I've made too much as usual," Mrs. Sutton explained, handing Mom the dish. "Lord knows, Henry doesn't need any extra helpings. You and Michael enjoy the chicken and potatoes and just relax tonight."

Mom tried to say no, but Mrs. Sutton insisted. "And you call me if you need anything else. You hear me?"

Mom managed a weak smile and nodded her head. Then she handed Michael the dish and gave Mrs. Sutton a hug. "You're a godsend, you know that?"

Back at their apartment, Michael put away his coloring book and went to wash his hands before dinner just as he did every night. He was still rinsing when he heard a terrible crash in the kitchen.

"Mama?" Michael called. There was no answer.

"*Mama*?"

Michael limped as fast as he could into the kitchen. Chicken and broken shards of Mrs. Sutton's dish were scattered across the floor. Mom was sitting doubled over in a chair. Her back was heaving up and down.

"Mama, what's wrong?" Michael cried out, terrified.

"Michael. Baby," Mom gasped. "I need you to...do something." Mom sat up, wheezed, and put her hand on her chest. Her face was twisted in pain—a look that he still saw sometimes in his worst nightmares.

"You...go...to Mrs. Sutton. Tell her..." Mom struggled for breath. "Tell her to call 911. Can you do that?"

Michael nodded.

"Hurry!"

Mrs. Sutton's apartment was only eight doors away, but to Michael it felt like a mile. He had tried to run, but his legs got tripped up. Halfway down the hall, he fell and then struggled to get back up and reach Mrs. Sutton's door.

"Mama said call 911!" Michael screamed as he banged on the door. "She said hurry!"

Mrs. Sutton appeared seconds later and squatted down in front of Michael, who was shaking so much he could barely speak.

"What is it, baby?" she asked.

"911," Michael blurted between choking sobs. "Mama!"

Mrs. Sutton ran down the hall to their apartment. Michael had left the door wide open.

"Donna!" Mrs. Sutton called. Michael struggled to follow her. He reached the door and she saw his mother doubled over and heaving. Mrs. Sutton grabbed the phone in the kitchen and called 911 as Michael watched in horror.

Why was Mom sweating like that? Why couldn't she breathe?

"They're on the way," Mrs. Sutton said calmly. She picked up a newspaper and began fanning Mom. "Don't you worry, now. Everything's gonna be okay. They'll be here any minute."

Michael went to put his arms around Mom's neck, but Mrs. Sutton nudged him away. "Not right now, baby. Give her some space."

"But what's *wrong*?" Michael asked through tears.

"I don't know," Mrs. Sutton said as she shook her head. "But people who can help her are on the way, Michael. It'll all be okay."

Michael hurried to his room and grabbed his stuffed giraffe. He clutched it tightly and watched from the hallway as Mrs. Sutton fanned Mom and whispered words of encouragement. Soon voices and footsteps echoed in the hallway. A man and a woman dressed in uniforms rushed into the apartment and attached wires and tubes to Mom. They quickly placed her on what looked like a tall bed on wheels. Mom was no longer gasping for breath. Maybe that meant she was better.

Michael limped into the kitchen to ask about Mom. Mr. Sutton had joined Mrs. Sutton, but no one was speaking. The uniformed man and woman didn't even look at them. Without a word, they rolled Mom out the door, down the long hallway and into the elevator.

Gone.

A siren wailed. Michael dropped the giraffe to the floor to cover his ears.

"Michael, you come and stay with us tonight, okay?" Mrs. Sutton said gently. Mr. and Mrs. Sutton each took one of Michael's hands and led him back to their apartment.

"When is Mama coming home?" Michael asked as he poked at the chicken dinner Mrs. Sutton put in front of him.

"Soon, sweetie," Mrs. Sutton said.

But Michael saw Mr. Sutton frown across the table at his wife.

An hour later, Mrs. Sutton's phone rang. She left the room to answer it, but Michael listened to every word.

"That can't be!" she said over and over again from her bedroom.

Mr. Sutton joined her in the other room, and they talked in low voices for so long that Michael finally got up and wandered into their bedroom too. Mrs. Sutton rushed over and hugged him the second he came in. When she put her cheek next to his, it felt damp.

Why was Mrs. Sutton crying?

"Oh, baby," she said, her voice cracking with each word. "I'm so sorry, Michael. Your mama…your poor mama…."

"What?" Michael asked. "What is it?"

Mr. Sutton sighed, put his hand on Michael's shoulder, and looked him in the eye.

"Son, your mother has passed away," he explained. "They said it was her heart. I know it's hard to understand, Michael, but her heart just gave out."

Michael stared at Mr. and Mrs. Sutton in confusion. What did that mean?

"Passed away?" Michael repeated, unable to understand. "What…where…?"

"Michael, your mama has died," Mr. Sutton finally said. "She had a heart attack, and they couldn't get her to the hospital in time. Son, we are so very sorry."

Died.

All Michael knew about death was that it was something bad that happened to other people. Not to Mama. His mother *couldn't* have died.

"*NO!*" Michael screamed. "Don't say that! It's not true! I want my Mama! Where is she?"

He broke free from Mrs. Sutton's arms and staggered to the sofa to grab his giraffe. He held it close, repeating *no, no, no,* over and over. Tears of fear and confusion spilled from his eyes.

Mr. and Mrs. Sutton rushed to his side, putting their arms around him in a circle.

"When is she coming back?" Michael asked between sobs. "You said she'd be back soon. You *said* so!"

Mrs. Sutton rubbed Michael's back and shook her head. "I'm sorry, baby. I was wrong. She isn't coming back. She's gone."

Three days later, Michael sat in a chair near the back of a crowded funeral home. The room was packed with people who spoke in low voices and kept looking at him with sad faces. Michael nibbled on a cookie Mrs. Sutton had given him and listened to what they were saying.

"Is there anyone left that can take care of him?" asked a man standing behind Michael.

"I think there's just his no-good father and an aunt," a nearby woman answered in a hushed voice that he recognized from church. They spoke as if he wasn't there and couldn't hear every word.

At one point, Michael stood up and stared at the people in the room. Was his father *here*? He limped around, looking up into the faces of all the men. Some of them smiled at him and gave him a hug or a friendly squeeze on his arm.

"Is my daddy here?" Michael asked Mrs. Sutton when he finally managed to reach her. She was standing in a small group of women, all of whom looked down at him with teary eyes. Some of them shook their heads slowly, and Michael thought a few of them seemed angry.

"No, honey, he's not here," Mrs. Sutton said as she squatted down in front of him and wiped crumbs off his face. "But your Aunt Nora is right over there. Do you want to go say hello?"

A sour-looking woman in a black-and-red hat that looked too big for her head turned toward him. Michael recognized her face. He had seen her a few times at family gatherings, though she lived on the other side of the city.

Even as a young child, Michael could tell that Mom and her sister did not get along. At their last family reunion, he'd overheard older relatives talking about it.

"I know Nora and Donna are sisters, but they couldn't be more different," an elderly aunt had said. Michael had been hiding under a picnic table eating cookies and listening to them.

"They're *half*-sisters," someone corrected. "But it's best not to talk about it because there's some bad blood there that goes way back."

It was an idea that puzzled Michael at the time. How could someone be a half-sister?

At that same party, he noticed Aunt Nora didn't smile when they met or seem interested in him at all. Then he heard her tell Mom that she was glad her own son was no longer a young child.

"Little boys are dirty, loud, and always in the way," Aunt Nora had said with a grunt of annoyance. "No way I'd ever want to deal with *that* again." Mom had just frowned in response.

But at the funeral home, Aunt Nora was different. She seemed unusually interested in seeing Michael. When their eyes met, she circled toward him with a strange, bitter smile on her face.

"Hello, Michael," she said in an odd, strained voice. "I was so sorry to hear about your mother and my dear sister."

For some reason, Michael backed away.

Aunt Nora glanced quickly around the room and cleared her throat. Again, the sour smile stretched across her face. She crouched down and leaned in close to him. Michael thought she smelled like old cheese.

"Guess what? You're gonna come and live with your Aunt Nora! What do you think about that?" she asked.

Live with Aunt Nora?

Michael didn't understand. Wasn't he just going to stay with Mr. and Mrs. Sutton, as he had been doing for the past few days? Michael looked helplessly at the adults gathered around him. He turned to Mrs. Sutton, but she just nodded in a reassuring way and patted Michael's shoulder.

Michael backed away another step and shook his head.

"No," he whispered.

Aunt Nora straightened up. She grinned as though Michael had said something funny. Then she put her hands on her hips and smiled harshly.

"Well, Michael, that's the way it's gonna have to be. *Someone* has to take care of you. You can't just be left alone."

Michael stared up at his aunt. Her eyes were steely and cold, nothing like Mom's. A sudden stab of sorrow pierced him as the memory of his mother's words echoed in his head.

As long as I have you and you have me, we'll never be alone.

Michael stood in the middle of the large gathering of people who smiled when he looked at them. Some continued to come over to say kind things and hug him.

But Michael no longer had his mother.

And he had never felt so alone.

Chapter 3

Michael was jolted out of his memories as he turned the corner and Bluford High came into view. The school towered over nearby businesses, making Michael feel smaller and even less sure of himself. Though the school year hadn't yet started, a few students sat on the steps that led to Bluford's main entrance. Michael watched them for a moment, feeling suddenly conflicted. He wanted to get past them without being noticed, but he also longed to join them and not be an outsider.

Glancing up and down the street, Michael caught his reflection in a nearby store window.

A wiry kid stared back at him. *Scared and skinny,* Michael thought, *and limping.*

Beneath his jacket, Michael wore a wrinkled gray T-shirt and a pair of old jeans. He also had on the scuffed, no-name basketball sneakers Aunt Nora made him buy at the thrift store. She never shopped anywhere for him but the cheapest places. That was okay with Michael. The more he faded into the background, the better things usually were for him. He hoped his dull clothes would help him avoid attention at Bluford.

As he neared the high school, Michael was relieved to see the students on the steps get up and go inside. With no one watching, he gripped the handrail and began an awkward sort of side-shuffle up the steps. When he was younger, the stairs at Aunt Nora's had been a struggle, but over the years, he had learned how to quickly pull himself up with his arm as he climbed.

Michael had just reached the top step when a girl emerged from the steel front doors. She had cinnamon skin and black-rimmed glasses and carried a cardboard box with the words *Bluford Cheerleading* written on it. Michael stopped and pretended to read the papers Aunt Nora had given him.

"Hi!" the girl said, her voice warm and cheerful. "You need help or anything?"

"Um, no," Michael said, embarrassed. "I'm just here to..." He flipped through the papers. "To take something to Ms. Spencer."

The girl set down the box and adjusted her glasses. "Oh! She's the principal. All you do is go straight through these doors and take your first left. The main office is right there. You can't miss it."

"Okay, thanks," Michael replied, waiting for the girl to leave so she wouldn't see his limp. Sometimes it bothered Michael more to have kind people feel bad about his limp than it did to have cruel people make fun of him.

"See ya!" the girl said with a smile. Then she picked up the box and bounded down the steps.

Michael took a deep breath and headed toward the main office. He could feel his heart beginning to thud as he made his way down the long corridor. Michael hadn't realized he would have to meet with the principal alone. When they had moved to the neighborhood last year, Aunt Nora and Michael met with the middle school principal once before the start of eighth grade. That principal, Mr. Herndon, assured Michael he would have no trouble fitting in and making new friends. His prediction was wrong, and Michael couldn't wait to leave the middle school and most of the people he knew there. At least Bluford was a fresh start.

"Can I help you?" asked a stern woman the second Michael entered the main office. She had a pen in her hand, and her phone was ringing steadily. A sign on her desk read, *Ms. Bader, School Secretary.*

"Yeah, I want to drop off some papers for Ms. Spencer. My name is Michael Tatem," he explained, holding the papers up so she could see. "My aunt told me—"

"Have a seat," the secretary snapped, nodding toward a row of chairs as she answered the phone.

Michael retreated to the nearest chair and wondered why he even needed to meet with the principal. Couldn't he just drop off the papers? Aside from his chat with Mr. Herndon, he had never spoken to any principal for more than a minute. Why did Bluford's principal need to see him?

"Okay, she's ready for you," said Ms. Bader, breaking his thoughts. "Go straight back."

Michael tried to hide his limp as he headed toward the principal's office. But before he reached it, a tall, dark-skinned woman with a powerful smile and wire-rimmed glasses met him at the door.

"Welcome to Bluford High," she said, beaming at him. "I'm Ms. Spencer, the school principal. And you're Michael?" She reached out a hand to shake his. He felt her eyes examining him, taking in his clothes and his leg.

"Yes, ma'am," he answered, shaking her hand. It was firm but warm.

She invited him to take a seat and asked for his forms. She explained that she had a few questions for him.

"Nobody with you today?" she asked. "Your aunt couldn't make it?"

"No, ma'am. She had to work," Michael said.

Ms. Spencer nodded and made some notes. "Michael, the reason I wanted to chat with you today is to discuss services that might interest you. You live six blocks away. Are you sure you want to walk to school this year?" she asked gently. "Students who live close usually walk, but if for any reason you want to ride the bus, we can arrange a pickup—"

"No," Michael huffed. "I walked here today. It's all good."

He imagined getting on a bus full of students staring at him and wondering what kind of problem he had that he couldn't even walk six blocks. Then he imagined limping and looking for an empty seat while everyone laughed or felt sorry for him. There was no way he was going to ride the bus.

"That's fine," Ms. Spencer said, again jotting down some notes. "It's just that your middle school file says that you have a problem with your leg. Could you tell me, Michael—if you don't mind—what the problem is?"

A hot wave of shame rolled through Michael's insides. He looked down at his trembling hands and then up at Ms. Spencer. He was surprised by what he saw. She seemed sincere and kind, something that Michael wasn't used to. Usually when people asked about his leg, they were either being nosy or mean. Most people didn't actually *care* about what was wrong.

"When I was little, I broke my leg in a bad way. I can't even remember it, really..." Michael began. Ms. Spencer's expression softened, and for a second it reminded him of his mother's face. Michael felt a sudden lump in his throat, and to his horror, his eyes began to sting with tears. "It...it never healed right," he stammered.

"Well, I'm sure all the walking won't make it any easier," Ms. Spencer said. "If you decide you'd rather take the bus, just let the office know. It'll be no problem at all."

Michael nodded and wiped his eyes quickly. He hoped she hadn't noticed his tears.

"So it says here you moved with your Aunt Nora into our district last year," Ms. Spencer continued, flipping through a folder on her desk. "Your records show you've always been a great student. I am happy to see that. How do you and your aunt like the new neighborhood?"

Michael shrugged. He wasn't sure what he was supposed to say. "I mean, we don't talk much, but it's fine, I guess," he admitted.

"Well, surely you talk sometimes, right?" Ms. Spencer said helpfully. Michael noticed a wrinkle of worry around her eyes. "Maybe at dinner once in a while?"

"I mean, we don't really eat together," Michael replied, hoping he was saying the right thing. "Way back when my cousin still lived with us, my aunt used to cook most nights but not anymore. Now she brings home leftovers from the cafeteria at the nursing home where she works."

Ms. Spencer's smile faded. She leaned in on her desk and folded her hands. Worried, Michael quickly added, "But it's not bad, though. I make sandwiches or microwave something for dinner when she doesn't bring anything. Some days she heats up soup or brings home chicken or whatever, and she even gives me money to get tacos down the street sometimes."

Ms. Spencer nodded and jotted something down on a piece of paper.

"I realize you're older now and may not do as much with your aunt as you used to, but when you were a child, what sorts of things did you two enjoy doing together?"

Michael was confused. Why was Ms. Spencer asking all this? The truth was, Aunt Nora had never done much of *anything* with him. When Michael was little, she had helped him get ready for school and introduced him to some of the neighborhood kids, but she never took him anywhere. Only Mrs. Sutton did that. She had stopped by often to take him to the movies or out for ice cream or to the nearby library. Otherwise, Michael spent most of his time at home alone. Michael tried explaining this to Ms. Spencer the best he could, but the more he said, the more she seemed to frown.

"But it's okay," Michael added quickly. "I go to the library, and I read a lot of books."

Ms. Spencer smiled briefly, but then she turned serious again.

"Has anyone ever checked on you to make sure you have everything you need?"

"Check on me?" Michael asked her. "Who would do that?"

"Sometimes when kids are in foster care or things are tough at home, a social worker or someone from DHS might drop by to make sure everything's okay."

Foster care? What does that have to do with me? Michael wondered. He had heard horror stories about foster care, and he couldn't imagine DHS or whoever coming to his apartment.

"She's my aunt, though, so why would they even come by?" Michael asked. "Besides, we're fine." Her questions were making him nervous. Why was she writing each time he talked?

"The thing is, Michael, someone at your middle school put a note in your file, and I just want to make sure everything's okay as you start out here at Bluford," she explained.

"A note? What kind of note?"

"It's about your leg, Michael," she admitted. "Has your aunt ever taken you to a doctor to have your leg looked at?"

"What…what do you mean?" Michael stammered, embarrassed. "I already told you. I broke it bad when I was little."

"Yes, but I can see that it still hurts you. So has your aunt had a doctor look at it?" Ms. Spencer repeated.

"No," Michael said with a shrug. "Aunt Nora doesn't like me complaining about my leg. She always says I'll outgrow it, and it'll heal when I'm older."

Ms. Spencer winced at his words, and for a split second, Michael thought he saw anger flash across her face. He wondered if he should leave. He didn't want the principal to dislike him.

A loud knock at the door interrupted them. Ms. Bader popped her head in and mentioned something about a meeting. Ms. Spencer thanked her, and then she stood up. Michael was glad her nosy questions were over. He stood as quickly as his leg would allow and headed toward the door, but Ms. Spencer stopped him with a hand on his shoulder.

"Thank you for your time today, Michael. I think you're gonna like it here," she said, the warm smile back on her face. "Many students have wonderful years at Bluford, and I want you to be one of them. We'll see you here when school begins on Monday morning!"

Michael nodded shyly and mumbled a thank-you. As he walked out, he tried to hide his limp, but when he passed by the front desk, he noticed Ms. Bader watching him. Was she already feeling sorry for him?

Just keep moving, Michael thought as he limped out into the hallway. He tried walking more quickly, which caused his leg to hurt more, but he desperately wanted to leave the school before anyone else saw him or asked questions. He was relieved when he reached the hallway and found it completely empty.

Almost there, Michael thought as he moved toward the main doors. A thin stream of sweat trickled down his face. Suddenly, a classroom door flew open, and out walked the girl who had been carrying the box earlier. She was with two other girls, all of them wearing *Bluford Cheerleading* T-shirts. Michael wished he could stop and hide his limp, but the girls were headed straight toward him. Stopping would only draw more attention. Michael put his head down and pretended not to notice the girls as they got closer.

"Hey! Did you find..." the girl with the glasses began in a friendly voice, but then her tone changed. Michael knew she had noticed his limp. "...Ms. Spencer's office?"

Michael glanced up for a second. "Yes. Thanks," he said quickly as he lurched toward the exit. But in that second, their eyes met. Michael saw it then, like a giant road sign in broad daylight, the thing he dreaded most: pity. As he passed them, Michael felt all three girls watching him and feeling sorry for him. It tore him up inside.

Pushing the doors open, he moved as quickly as he could down the steps in a jerky sideways motion. A small group of older boys at the bottom watched Michael struggling.

"You okay, bro?" someone asked as Michael reached the last step.

Michael kept his head down and lumbered past them without a word.

Back on the street, he finally raised his head. It was a busy time of day, and everyone seemed to have somewhere to go, something to do, someone to meet. Friends walked together, talking and laughing. Horns honked, and music spilled out of windows. No one seemed to notice the fourteen-year-old wearing old clothes and limping along the sidewalk.

The entire world rushed around Michael, completely unaware that he existed.

And for the first time that day, Michael felt relief.

Chapter 4

On Monday morning, Michael felt sick with nervousness. He skipped breakfast and slipped out the front door an hour early, hoping he could get to Bluford before the packed buses arrived. Michael knew that it would be only a matter of time before the entire school would know him as "that kid with the limp." But on this very first morning, he hoped to avoid kids gawking at him as he struggled up the steps.

Michael kept his eyes down and his hands shoved in his pockets as he made his way toward the high school. In his right hand, he held a smooth black stone that he turned over and over.

Not long before his mother had died, Michael had taken a ride with her to the beach. They had sat near the surf together playing in the sand when Mom had found the black stone.

"Wow! How'd it get so smooth and shiny?" he had asked, examining it closely.

"It has been tumbling in the ocean for years, getting tossed and turned. But you see? The waves and sand didn't destroy it. It just kept getting smoother and more beautiful all by itself. It's like you," Mom had said as she handed it to Michael. "You're like this stone. Each day only makes you stronger and more beautiful. Don't you ever let anyone make you feel bad about yourself. You hear me?"

Michael gripped the stone tightly as he approached Bluford. He was relieved to see only a few students hanging out near the entrance when he arrived. No one seemed to watch as he climbed the steps. He paused against the railing at the top step as the street filled with cars and buses. Soon throngs of noisy students were pouring into the high school. Michael waited until the crowd was so thick and slow-moving that no one could tell he had a limp.

"Good morning, Michael. Welcome!" a familiar voice called out cheerfully.

Michael spotted Ms. Spencer just inside the door, greeting as many students as she could. Her smile seemed to fade slightly when she glanced down to his worn shoes and then back up to his face. Michael realized he was wearing the same dull jeans and gray T-shirt he had on the day he met her. All around him, students wore bright new school clothes and expensive, brand-name shoes. Some carried new phones too. Michael couldn't imagine what it was like to own such things. His aunt had never allowed it, though she always seemed to have new things of her own.

In his first class, English, Michael moved carefully to the back of the classroom and sat down quickly in his seat. The only student who seemed to notice his limping was the girl who sat right in front of him. Everyone else appeared to be so busy looking at their phones or chatting with each other that, much to Michael's relief, they paid no attention to him.

The teacher, a tall Black man wearing a purple button-down shirt with a bright green and purple tie, smiled cheerfully as he entered the classroom, but Michael looked away. As the room steadily filled, he recognized a few students from middle school: Marcia Lopez, a cute girl who always ignored him. Nelson Green, a boy who always seemed tired and bored, even at lunch. And, to Michael's dismay, Brandon Miller, a kid who had never missed an opportunity to tease Michael last year. Even though it was the first day of school, Brandon swaggered into the classroom as if he owned it.

Michael felt a jolt of anxiety shoot through him. Brandon was big for his age—and he seemed to have grown even taller over the summer. His favorite pastime in eighth grade was making life miserable for kids who were different. Brandon had targeted Michael many times, giving him the name "Speedy." He used it so often that Michael sometimes wondered if Brandon even knew his real name.

Recalling what happened last year, Michael instinctively grabbed the stone in his pocket. He remembered the warm Friday last May when Brandon had come up behind him in the middle school hallway and slapped him on his back as if they were friends.

"How's it going, Speedy?" he had asked, with a broad smile.

Michael had been confused at first. He wondered if Brandon had finally finished being mean to him. Maybe he wanted to put that behind them.

"Pretty good," Michael had replied, confused but hopeful.

"Great!" Brandon said with another friendly pat on the back. Then he hurried down the hallway.

Not long afterward, Michael heard laughter behind him and noticed students turning around to grin at him whenever he passed by. Finally, in health class, a student behind him tapped him on the shoulder and said, "Yo, Michael, you got something on your back."

That's when Michael reached around and discovered a piece of paper had been taped to him. Scrawled in bright red marker, it said, *Wanna Race?*

Now as Michael watched Brandon saunter into their English class, a familiar mix of shame and anger bubbled up inside him. He ducked his head to keep from being seen and was glad when Brandon chose a desk up front.

"All right, let's get your first class at Bluford High started! I'm Mr. Mitchell," the teacher announced. "For today, I'd like you to get to know each other, so here's what we're going to do. I'll pair each of you up with a person near you. You'll have fifteen minutes to find out three interesting facts about your classmate. Then everyone will take turns coming up front and introducing their partner to the class."

Grumbling erupted from throughout the room.

"Tell me he ain't serious," mumbled someone from the back of the room.

"Oh, I'm serious all right," Mr. Mitchell said with a grin. He then held his hand up for quiet and added, "In this class, I expect participation from everyone. Speaking up and sharing your thoughts is as important as any test in here. Think of these introductions as icebreakers. And don't worry about being nervous. Nervousness just means that you care about what you're doing."

Michael felt his heart throbbing like a drum in his chest. He was beyond nervous—he was terrified. Stepping to the front of the classroom with twenty-five students watching his every move was his worst nightmare. As Mr. Mitchell began pairing up students, Michael eyed the door. Could he just leave somehow? Maybe if he…

"Hi, I'm Zoe."

The voice startled him from his thoughts. Michael turned to see that the girl in front of him had turned completely around to face him. Her almond eyes were locked on his. The classroom suddenly began to buzz with the laughter and chatter of nearby students.

"Uh, hi. I'm…I'm Michael," he said, looking down as he struggled to find the right words. He realized there was no way to escape Mr. Mitchell's assignment, yet he was sure it would end in disaster. Like a protective reflex, Michael shoved his hand into his pocket and gripped Mom's stone again.

"If you want, you can go first," Zoe offered. Her voice seemed friendly and almost musical. "I'm gonna write down what you say so I don't forget when I get in front of the class."

Zoe cringed for a second as if the idea of speaking in front of everyone bothered her too. Michael nodded but avoided looking directly at her. He wasn't used to talking to girls, especially cute girls like Zoe. He had no idea what to say or where to begin. He couldn't even think of one thing that was interesting about himself.

"I guess you could tell me what hobbies you have," Zoe suggested. "Where you live, what you like to do. Stuff like that."

Michael rubbed his cheek and searched for answers. "I live with my aunt 'cause my mom died of a heart attack when I was six. You can just say I live with my aunt."

Zoe's eyes widened. "Oh, wow. I'm really sorry," she said. She reached over and touched his desk as she spoke, which made Michael look up at her. He knew the pity in her eyes wasn't because of his leg, but it still made him feel hurt and angry in a way he couldn't understand. He looked away from Zoe and folded his arms.

"And…I like to read books from the library. And…and…I collect beach rocks," Michael added quickly.

The last part wasn't exactly true, but in the handful of times Michael had gone to the beach with Mrs. Sutton since his mom died, he had found three more smooth, shiny stones. He kept them lined up on his windowsill and often picked them up and looked at them. The rocks gave him an odd sense of peace.

Zoe finished jotting down her notes. "Okay. Anything else?" she asked.

Michael shook his head. He knew that Zoe had seen him limping when he walked to his desk, but he wasn't about to mention that. "No. Your turn. What about you?"

"Well, let's see," Zoe began. She scrunched up her face as if she were lost in thought for a moment. Michael noticed her tightly curled hair and how it spilled along her face, down her neck, and onto her shoulders. She wore a striped T-shirt, and just above the V-neck he spotted a thin gold chain with a hanging *Z*. He suddenly became aware of his worn shoes and dull clothes.

"Okay. So my dad moved here from Tanzania sixteen years ago, so I'm half Tanzanian."

Michael wasn't sure how to spell *Tanzania*, so he scribbled down something that looked like the word.

"And I like adopting stray pets, but my parents don't like it very much."

Zoe paused and smiled, but Michael was so worried about walking to the front of the room that all he managed to jot down on his paper was "stray pets."

"And I guess you could also say that I like to invent new kinds of cookies. Last week, I made some peanut-butter-and-strawberry cookies. I know that sounds weird, but they were really good."

Michael wrote down as much as he could, though his hands were trembling so much that his own handwriting looked strange to him. When he finally looked up, he noticed Zoe watching him expectantly.

"So, you ready?" she asked with a smile.

"Yeah, sure," Michael mumbled.

The room had grown so loud with conversation that Mr. Mitchell had to clap his hands to quiet down the class. Michael couldn't imagine actually *enjoying* doing this. Nearly everyone else looked excited, but Michael wished he could just disappear.

"Okay, we'll begin over here," Mr. Mitchell said, pointing to the first student on the left. One by one, students came up and introduced one another. Mr. Mitchell made welcoming comments to each student, but to Michael, it all seemed to be happening in a haze. A dull pounding began in Michael's head. It wasn't until Zoe stood up to introduce Michael that he realized the booming was his heart. As Zoe repeated what Michael had told her, the entire classroom turned to look at him. Michael felt a wave of heat roll into his face, and his mouth was suddenly as dry as paper.

"Ah, a patron of the library! Good for you, Michael," Mr. Mitchell said, nodding at him approvingly. "Your turn," the teacher urged, motioning for Michael to come to the front of the class.

Michael gripped the side of his desk to steady himself as he stood up. His limbs suddenly felt weak and rubbery. With his heart pounding like a hammer, Michael limped awkwardly to the front of the room.

Students on both sides of him craned their necks to look down at his feet. Someone near the back snickered. Brandon shook his head and grinned malevolently.

"I…I'm introducing…" Michael began. He looked down at the crumpled piece of paper in his shaking hand. "Um…I…" Michael suddenly realized he had forgotten to write down her full name, and now, with everyone's eyes on him, he couldn't remember it. Looking over at her in desperation, Michael blurted out, "What's your name again?"

The entire class erupted in laughter. Even Mr. Mitchell chuckled before telling everyone to quiet down.

Overcome with shame, Michael barely made it through the rest of the introduction. He mistakenly said Zoe was *Tasmanian* instead of *Tanzanian*, and then, because his handwriting was so messy, he accidentally said that she liked to adopt stray *pots,* not pets. That created another outburst of laughter. Brandon, who was sitting directly in front of Michael, sneered at him.

"Way to go, Speedy," he mumbled just loud enough for Michael, but no one else, to hear. When it was over, Michael limped back to his desk in utter humiliation.

"It's okay," Zoe whispered as Michael went by. But Michael couldn't bear to look at her. He sat down heavily and sank as low as he could go.

I hate being here, he thought miserably. *I hate being me*.

Chapter 5

The rest of Michael's first day at Bluford High did not get any better.

The last class of the morning was gym, and Michael had been dreading it more than any other class on his schedule. Last year in middle school, Ms. Worrell didn't notice his limp on the first day and tried to assign him to play soccer with the whole class. By the time she realized her mistake, everyone was staring at Michael's odd leg as if it carried a disease they could catch.

Fearing a repeat of that day, Michael limped into the gym and took a seat on the bleachers near where students were lining up for class. Someone made a snorting noise as Michael hobbled past. "I'll bet he can play some serious hoops," another mumbled. Michael pretended not to hear them.

Just then a stocky man in a navy *Bluford High School* sweatshirt hurried over and introduced himself as Mr. Dooling, the gym teacher. A silver whistle hung from his neck, and he carried a shiny clipboard.

"We're going to get started today by doing some stretches and some easy running, so everybody go get changed, and let's get at it!" Mr. Dooling barked. Then he blew the whistle and pointed toward the locker room.

Easy running? Michael thought, feeling panic rise in him. *This can't be happening!*

Suddenly, Mr. Dooling blew his whistle a second time as he stared at his clipboard. "Hold up a second," he shouted. "Michael Tatem and Joe Davis. Front and center. I need to talk to you."

Everyone watched as Michael limped over to Mr. Dooling. Joe, a tall boy who looked completely bored, also walked toward the gym teacher.

"All right, Michael and Joe," Mr. Dooling said in a voice that Michael wished was not so loud. "You two are excused from this class due to your health issues. Starting Wednesday, you'll take study hall instead. For today and tomorrow, you can have a seat in the bleachers."

Mortified that everyone was still staring at him, Michael limped back to where he had been sitting. Joe sat nearby. "I have bad asthma," he explained with a lazy shrug. "I could probably do most of the stuff in here, but my parents won't let me."

When Michael didn't reply, Joe added, "I mean it's not like I can't run."

Michael looked away. For the second time that day, he wished he could just disappear.

At lunch, Michael discovered that the only empty tables were in the far corners of the cafeteria. He didn't mind eating alone, but he wished there was someplace closer to sit. He spotted a few empty seats at a nearby table and quickly sat down.

"Nah, I don't think so," grumbled a kid sitting on the opposite end of the table. "This here table is *reserved*."

Michael glanced up to see four older boys glaring back at him. The one who spoke wore a tight *Los Angeles Rams* T-shirt that showed off his muscled arms and broad shoulders.

"Well, what are you waitin' for?" the boy asked. "Move on, bro."

Michael limped away as fast as he could, but his tray teetered with each of his awkward, jerky steps. While he fought to steady his plate of pizza, an apple slipped off his tray and rolled between two tables as students watched. Michael pretended not to notice and just kept moving.

"Hey!" someone shouted. "Ya want your apple back?"

Michael turned to see a group of girls grinning at him. One held his apple up in the air like a baseball.

"Catch!" she yelled and tossed the apple in his direction.

With his hands holding his tray, Michael had no way to catch anything. Instead, he flinched and ducked, and the apple sailed past him. It landed on a backpack at another table, where a guy snatched it up and threw it to a friend. Embarrassed, Michael moved away from the commotion and found an empty table where he could turn his back to everyone. He stared at his tray of food. He hadn't eaten all day, and the pizza looked good, but he was no longer hungry.

After lunch, Michael's last two classes were up two flights of stairs. Michael knew there had to be an elevator somewhere, but he also knew using it would make him stand out. With so many students in the hallways, Michael figured he could just mix in with the crowd and move up the steps unnoticed. But it didn't quite work out that way.

Michael rushed to pull himself along the stair railing with his right arm, but it wasn't nearly as fast as the students behind him wanted to walk. Soon people began yelling at him.

"What's the holdup?"

"C'mon, man. *Move*!"

"Seriously, you're gonna make me late for class."

Michael tried to go faster, but then he dropped his notebook. It slapped to the ground behind him, but there was no way he could turn around to grab it. He tried to see where it had gone as students pushed and jostled past him. Then someone stepped on his foot while someone else shouldered him aside. For a split second, Michael felt himself slip and thought he might fall when suddenly a strong hand gripped his arm. He looked up and was surprised to see a familiar face. Cooper nodded and helped Michael up the rest of the stairs without a word. When they reached the top, he handed Michael his notebook.

"Hey...thanks," Michael said, feeling equally relieved and embarrassed.

"No problem, bro," Cooper said with a smile. "People are crazy the first few days, trying to find their classes and figure out their lockers. It's gonna be all right. You'll see."

Then with a friendly shoulder slap, Cooper turned and disappeared into the crowd.

Two hours later, Michael's first day at Bluford was over, but the six-block walk to Aunt Nora's still remained. Michael waited until most students were gone before he made his way home. A half-block from the apartment, he heard the heavy rumble of a big vehicle. Michael turned to see a yellow school bus screech to a stop alongside him. Several students inside stared down at him. Then a window snapped open, and a familiar face poked out.

"Yo, Speedy!"

It was Brandon. Michael clenched his teeth and kept moving. His apartment was across the street. Just a few more steps, and he could escape inside and shut the world out.

"I'm talking to you, Speedy," Brandon shouted again.

Laughter poured from the bus as it began moving again. Michael glanced back to see Brandon pointing and sneering. "Don't wear your legs out looking for... STRAY POTS!"

Michael could still hear Brandon cackling as the bus pulled away. Fighting back angry tears, he limped inside his building, unlocked the door to his apartment, and rushed down the narrow hallway to his room. A sliver of afternoon sunlight beamed through the window and made the rocks on his windowsill sparkle. Michael reached into his pocket, pulled out the smooth black stone that Mom had given him, and wept.

Always remember that you're as strong and beautiful as this stone, she had told him.

But as Michael stared at his reflection in the small mirror by his bed, he looked neither strong nor beautiful. Tears streaked his face. He felt weak and sad and alone.

Michael remembered his mother's words, but at that moment, he did not believe them.

Later that night, Michael lay awake worrying about how he would get through the first week at Bluford, much less four years. But as he lay there listening to the creaking of water pipes, it occurred to him that he had lived with his aunt for twice that long. And as bad as things often were with her, the years had gone by quickly. Like a movie unwinding in his head, Michael thought back to his first memories of moving in with Aunt Nora so many years ago.

He had arrived at her house on Raymond Street heartbroken after losing Mom. At the time, Aunt Nora's son Trevon was still living at home. Even though Trevon was fourteen and forced to share his room with his sad six-year-old cousin, he wasn't unkind to Michael.

"Man, I'm really sorry about your mom," Trevon said that first night. He even shook Michael's hand and surprised him by giving him a piece of gum, though it was late.

Aunt Nora had set up a cot for Michael to sleep on, but he had trouble sleeping at first. Homesick, scared, and lonely, Michael would often cry quietly for hours.

"It's gonna be all right, cuz," Trevon had said from across the room the first few nights. But one night, when Michael's sobbing had grown too loud, Trevon woke up and turned on the light.

"You've got to get over this, Michael," Trevon said somewhat impatiently. Then he added in a kinder voice, "Things'll get better, but you've gotta go to sleep now."

For a time, Michael learned to muffle his crying by pulling a pillow over his head. But gradually he cried less and less. Sometimes, Trevon would let Michael play Minecraft on his phone or just sit and talk with him until he got drowsy. Eventually, Michael was able to sleep through the night.

That first year, Aunt Nora made sure that everything was set for Michael to start first grade. She introduced him to the neighbors on both sides of her house. Each family had children around Michael's age. After school and on weekends, the kids played together out front. Everyone was curious about Michael's limp, but no one was ever mean to him. Even so, he often felt embarrassed whenever he played with them. He was always slower and less skilled than everyone else, and nothing he could do would change that.

Even back then, Aunt Nora was never warm or loving toward Michael. On evenings when the three of them would eat dinner, she would mostly just watch TV or browse her phone, ignoring Michael and only occasionally speaking to Trevon. At first, Michael had tried to join in their conversations or ask Aunt Nora questions, but she usually just dismissed him or ignored him. Sometimes she would get annoyed and snap.

"There you go again acting like you're special. You're just like your mother. Always got something to say even though no one asked you."

In those early days, Michael missed Mom more than ever, especially her hugs—something Aunt Nora never provided. Sometimes, the mothers of his next-door playmates would come outside and hug their own children, and Michael would stare at them. He couldn't help it.

"You need a hug too, baby?" the moms would ask. They would even reach down to put their arms around him, but it was never enough. There was an emptiness in Michael, a void so vast that it ached like a wound. More than once, when sitting in his first-grade classroom, Michael would think of Mom, feel the pain, and begin crying.

"What's wrong, Michael?" his teacher, Ms. Garcia, asked one day. It was just before Mother's Day, and everyone was making cards for their mothers. Everyone but him.

Michael wrapped his arms around himself and rocked in his desk at the back of the classroom. "I hurt," he said.

Mrs. Henry, the school nurse, had gotten used to seeing him that year. She would let him come to the office whenever he needed to cry and hug him until he felt better. Sometimes he would head back to class in just a few minutes, but other times it took longer.

"You're grieving, baby," she had said each time he came to her. "Let it out. It's okay."

In spite of his occasional bouts of sorrow, Michael gradually grew to enjoy elementary school. He worked hard and learned to read, listened to his teachers, and raised his hand to answer questions. He knew it was what his mother would have wanted—she loved books and learning, too. Because of his limp, Michael was often timid around his classmates, but he still managed to make some friends. Out on the playground, Darius, his next-door neighbor and best friend, made sure no one picked on Michael.

"Michael doesn't have to play, but he can watch us," Darius would say whenever a group of kids began playing tag or football.

But the greatest source of happiness in Michael's life during the first years he lived with Aunt Nora was visits from his old babysitter, Mrs. Sutton. Aunt Nora never liked having her around, and she glared at Mrs. Sutton with sour impatience if she ever stayed for more than an hour. Even so, Mrs. Sutton managed to fill her visits with cookies, books, and endless hugs. Best of all, she introduced Michael to the nearby library, and she helped him get his very own library card.

"This card is like a magic ticket," Mrs. Sutton had said with a grin as she handed it to Michael. "All you gotta do is show it to the librarian, and you can get books to read for free! And there are libraries all over the city. No matter where you are, you can find one nearby."

For nearly four years, life with Aunt Nora was bearable—sometimes even good. But around the time Michael entered fifth grade, everything began to change.

Arguments between Aunt Nora and Trevon became louder and more frequent. One day, out of the blue, Trevon pulled out an old suitcase, slammed it on his bed, and announced that he was moving in with a friend until he could join the Army.

Michael watched as Trevon packed his bag in tense silence. When he was done, Trevon sat on his bed and looked Michael in the eye. "I know I shouldn't say this, but you ain't nothing but a monthly check to my mom. She don't care about what happens to you or me. All she cares about is herself."

"What…what do you mean?" Michael asked. How could a mother not care about her own son?

Trevon sighed, and a dark sadness filled his eyes. "It's a long story, but my mom's got a lot of anger. I get that, but it don't give her a right to take it out on me. She told me more than once that I was just a mistake. I never knew my dad, but I know she hates him. I figure that's why she hates me."

"She doesn't hate you," Michael said, trying to find some way to comfort him.

Trevon shrugged and shook his head. Anger replaced the sadness in his eyes. They sat together in the quiet room for a long moment. Then a car honked outside. Trevon stood up and put his hand on Michael's shoulder for the last time.

"Take care of yourself, cuz," Trevon said, shaking his head. "You got a rough time ahead of you, if you know what I mean."

At first, Michael hadn't understood what Trevon was talking about. But it wasn't long before he came to know exactly what Trevon meant.

Chapter 6

"There are gonna be some changes around here," Aunt Nora announced the day Trevon left four years ago.

"You got a whole room to yourself now," Aunt Nora snapped, glaring at him. "From now on, when I'm here, I expect you to stay in there. Don't be thinking you can just hang out downstairs when I'm relaxing or whatever. You keep to yourself and give me my space. You understand?"

Michael nodded and backed away from his aunt. She tossed mail addressed to Trevon into the kitchen trash can and slammed her phone on the counter.

"And don't you ever mention Trevon around me, you hear? I don't need him or anybody," she huffed as Michael escaped to his room.

Over the next few weeks, Aunt Nora made it clear that there were only certain times he was allowed to be in the kitchen or bathroom. With Trevon gone, Michael was to eat his meals alone. She kept bread, bologna, peanut butter, and jelly in the kitchen for him to make lunches on non-school days. A jug of milk and a huge box of no-name corn flakes was usually the only choice for breakfast. Increasingly, Aunt Nora ate dinner out. Sometimes she would come home dressed nicely and smelling like perfume. On those nights, Michael made boxed macaroni and cheese or canned soup or whatever else he could find. No matter what he ate, Michael wound up sitting alone in the kitchen with a book while Aunt Nora was in the living room relaxing. After he finished, he had to wash his dishes and retreat upstairs without a word to his aunt.

He was also given chores that Trevon had handled before. One was to take the trash to the curb every Sunday night. One time, he forgot, and Aunt Nora noticed it after she returned home late from an evening out. She hollered upstairs, waking him from a deep sleep. "Michael, get your butt down here and take out this trash!"

He stumbled downstairs in confusion.

"You missed trash pickup!" she fumed at him. "Now you're gonna take them bags over to the dumpster behind SuperFoods. Maybe you won't forget next time."

SuperFoods, a big supermarket, was three blocks away, and it took Michael two trips to haul all the bags to the dumpster. A group of older teenagers sitting in a car in the store parking lot laughed out loud at the sight of him dragging a big bag of garbage.

"Whatchu doing out here dumping trash in the middle of the night, little man?" one of them shouted. "You got a body in there or something?"

"Someone needs to get that boy a shopping cart—or a wheelchair!" another snorted.

Even though it was years ago, Michael remembered the night as if it were yesterday.

Around that same time, Mrs. Sutton began visiting Michael less frequently. Weeks went by without her appearing. Then one day she visited and had a tear-filled talk with him.

"Michael, you know I love seeing you." She sat next to him and took his hands in hers as she spoke. "But I'm not going to be able to visit anymore. Mr. Sutton is very sick now; he needs me nearby all the time, and I just can't be all the way across the city. I hope you can understand."

Michael stared at Mrs. Sutton. He felt as if the last bit of light inside him was being snuffed out.

"You're a good boy," Mrs. Sutton continued, patting her eyes with a tissue. "Remember that, and remember that you were the sunshine in your mama's life. Now, listen—you have a library card, and the library is only a few blocks away, so you keep going there. Your mother would want you to."

Michael nodded and told Mrs. Sutton he would be okay, even as he fought back tears.

As it turned out, Michael began spending even more time than he wanted to at the library. Aunt Nora told him that he was old enough to stay out of the house during the day on weekends.

"With Trevon gone, this is *my* time," Aunt Nora had said. "I work all week caring for ungrateful people. I don't need you here disturbing things and crowding my kitchen. You got your friends, and you got the library. You find something to do until five o'clock."

This began Michael's middle school weekend routine. On Saturdays and Sundays, he would pack sandwiches and spend nearly all of his time in the library. Sometimes when the weather was nice, he imagined going to the park and staying outside, but the park was often crowded on weekends, and he didn't want to deal with dogs tripping him, little kids staring, or older ones teasing. At the library, he could disappear behind bookshelves and avoid everyone—most of the time. But one Sunday afternoon, a librarian noticed him.

"Is everything okay?" asked the librarian, a middle-aged white woman with graying curls. She peered at him through thick glasses. "I see you here a lot."

Michael nervously pointed to a stack of books next to him. "I just like to read. I mean, like all the time," he explained. "And...and it's quieter here than at home."

The librarian nodded and smiled. She left him alone after that.

Around this same time, many of Michael's neighborhood friends became more distant. The boys started leaving him behind when they got together to hang out. And the girls now seemed to look right through him when Michael was headed in their direction. Even Darius, Michael's closest friend, stopped spending time with him. Michael couldn't understand why at first. But then one day after school, he saw Darius talking to Felicia, a girl in their class. When Michael began limping toward the two of them, Darius turned his back as if he didn't see him. He then walked away with his arm around Felicia.

So that's how it is, Michael thought bitterly.

He knew the boys in his grade were getting interested in girls, but he hadn't expected his friends to dump him.

"Don't you like *anyone* at school?" Darius had asked a few weeks earlier. "Not even Felicia? That girl is *all that*."

Michael had shrugged. It wasn't that he hadn't noticed the girls in his class; it was just that he figured they wouldn't be interested in him. Who would want to be seen with a skinny guy with a bad limp?

No girl, Michael thought gloomily. *Ever.*

So as Michael moved through middle school, he spent even more time alone. Most days he limped around Aunt Nora's apartment as quietly as possible. On rare weekends when he didn't go to the library, he felt completely trapped. Summers were the worst. Then, Michael endured the silent nothingness of the empty apartment, while outside he could hear kids playing, music thumping in nearby apartments, and teens passing by on skateboards and bikes he could not ride.

Once, Michael looked down from his bedroom window and saw Darius walking hand-in-hand with Felicia, then stopping on the corner to kiss. Watching them only sharpened his loneliness. Sometimes the only sound Michael seemed to hear was the whisper of turning pages in whatever book he was reading.

Days could go by without Aunt Nora even speaking to him, but Michael preferred that to her complaining about him being in her way. He feared the cold looks she often gave him for being around, and he worried about what new changes she might have in store for him. Over time, he learned to hide his feelings and keep his expression calm and detached, a blank page, whenever she glared at him—just as he did with strangers who made fun of his limp. That way, Michael hoped, Aunt Nora might believe that her cruelty had no effect on him, that he was bulletproof and invulnerable.

But the truth was that the silence roared in his ears, and his aunt's meanness always hurt. Michael often felt the weight of his aloneness crushing him, creating a sharp pain beneath his ribs. He kept hoping that he could learn to live with it, the way he had learned to live with the pain in his leg. Or maybe Aunt Nora could soften and change? He hoped and prayed for it often, but it never came.

One Saturday evening, Michael smelled the aroma of fried catfish and browned potatoes drifting from the kitchen. It was around eight o'clock, and the smell was so delicious, Michael couldn't resist it. He decided to creep to the kitchen to grab a quick snack. He knew not to say a word to his aunt, but to his horror, he discovered she was not alone.

The small table had been set up for a fancy dinner. A wine bottle, two glasses, two plates, and a large salad bowl had been neatly arranged, making the apartment seem special and inviting. Aunt Nora was seated, her back to Michael. But opposite her, staring right at him, was a large man with a shiny bald head.

"Who's that?" the man exclaimed, putting down his glass and looking at Michael as if he had seen a ghost.

Aunt Nora turned and scowled at Michael, barely containing the rage in her eyes.

"Is that...your *son*? You never said you had a kid, Nora."

"I don't, Corey. That's Michael. He's my nephew. He's been living with me since his mama died—"

"But you *do* have a son," Michael blurted, the words coming out before he could even think to stop them. "What about Trevon?"

"Trevon?" the man said, his face twisted in confusion. "Who's he talking about? Why didn't you mention all this to me when I asked a while back if you had kids?"

"What'd I say to you about staying out of my space?!" Aunt Nora fumed, ignoring the man and aiming her fury straight at Michael, like a laser beam. "Get to your room. *Now!*"

Michael retreated, but as he left, he saw Corey stand up from the table and throw down his napkin. When Michael reached his room, he could hear his aunt straining to control what had just happened.

"Don't go, baby. I know kids aren't your thing, so I didn't want to mention it," Michael heard his aunt say. "Besides, my son is grown and gone, and Michael means nothing to me." The words hit Michael like daggers.

Corey left a short time later and never came back, but Aunt Nora's cruel words—and her resentment—never faded.

Though it was years ago, Michael lay awake a long time thinking about all that happened before he had arrived at Bluford. As hard as things had been in middle school, moving last year had been even worse. Aunt Nora never explained why they had to pack up and go so quickly. But Michael wondered if it had something to do with the increasing number of letters from his school and her being unable to afford repairs needed on her old house. When he tried to ask Aunt Nora why they were moving, she had gotten irritated.

"None of your business," she had snapped. "But you're gonna be going to high school in another year, and Bluford High is supposed to be one of the best in the city. So I don't want to hear any complaining. You ought to feel lucky to be moving."

But Michael didn't feel lucky. He had lost his old neighbors and friends. Instead, he had Brandon Miller and a bunch of strangers who barely spoke to him. The only bit of brightness was the small branch library nearby. It was actually closer than the one in his old neighborhood, and Michael was relieved to discover that the library card Mrs. Sutton had gotten for him worked there too. But Michael desperately missed the familiar faces and the occasional kind words from the neighbors he had known since he was a little kid. Like everything else he cared about, they were taken from him.

Michael shut his eyes, but sleep would not come. As he listened to a far-off siren, he realized that loneliness was not like the pain in his leg.

He could never get used to living with it.

Chapter 7

After a restless night, Michael awoke on Tuesday morning with a jolt. Somewhere down the block, a car alarm was honking and whooping. As he lay in his dim room dreading the day ahead, Michael decided that there was no point getting to Bluford an hour early. Even if he arrived at dawn every single day, he realized he could not stop everyone at school from knowing him as the crippled kid. There was no escape.

When Michael got to Bluford, Ms. Spencer was again greeting students as they walked through the front doors. Michael hoped he could slip by her unseen. But just as he passed, she placed her hand on his shoulder.

"Good morning, Michael," she said softly. "Before you leave school today, I want you to stop by my office. I have a note for you to give to your aunt."

"Okay," Michael answered, trying to hide the pang of nervousness he suddenly felt. Was he in trouble? No one ever had to take a note home from the principal unless there was something wrong. Michael's mind was racing so fast that he barely noticed the stares from other students as he limped toward Mr. Mitchell's English class.

"Everyone please take the same seat you had yesterday," Mr. Mitchell instructed as the classroom filled. Michael was relieved to be able to sit in the back row again, but just as he reached his seat, he saw Brandon heading toward him with a sneer on his face. Brandon slammed his books on the desk where Zoe sat yesterday.

"What's up, Speedy?" he scoffed, pulling off his earbuds.

"You can't sit there." Michael struggled to keep his voice calm.

"Why not?" Brandon challenged. He leaned toward Michael and grinned spitefully. "You gonna kick me out with your sideways foot?"

Brandon was facing the back of the room. Michael knew he could not see the teacher eyeing him and shaking his head.

"Brandon, your seat is up here," Mr. Mitchell declared, pointing to the seat Brandon sat in yesterday. "And please remove your earphones *before* coming to class, so you can hear what I'm saying."

Brandon sucked his teeth and mumbled something Michael couldn't hear. Zoe came flying through the door just as Brandon retreated from her desk.

"Whew! I thought for sure I was gonna be late," she said to Michael after she darted to her seat.

Michael wasn't sure how to respond. He felt shy in her gaze. After his embarrassing introduction yesterday, he was surprised she was even speaking to him.

"You still got like two minutes," Michael finally said, pointing at the clock on the side wall. "Brandon should call you Speedy instead of me."

"Ignore him," Zoe huffed. Then she opened her bookbag and grabbed a notebook and smiled. "So, you know anything about Mr. Mitchell? I heard that he's pretty good. But you also have to do the work. He doesn't let up on you if you don't."

Michael couldn't believe Zoe was actually talking to him. He felt a strange, unexpected rush of happiness.

"To be honest, I kind of like teachers like that," Michael admitted nervously.

"Me too!" Zoe beamed. "Sometimes my friends think I'm crazy, but I don't care. I'd rather be challenged than be bored."

Michael felt his pulse quicken. He knew what it was like to be challenged. He lived it every day. What he didn't know was how it felt to have a friend, especially a girl friend, who could relate to him. That was completely new.

"I don't think that's crazy," he replied, feeling both nervous and excited. "I feel the same way!"

"So then maybe we're both crazy." She laughed, extending her fist to him playfully. Michael bumped it gently with his, just as Mr. Mitchell began class.

For several long minutes, Michael could barely hear the teacher over the sound of his own racing heart.

At lunchtime, Michael returned to his familiar spot at the back of the cafeteria and discovered nearly every table was full. The one he had sat at the day before was occupied by three older guys talking about an upcoming football game. *Are they seniors?* Michael wondered. He was looking for another table when the guy closest to him nodded and said, "'Sup."

Relieved, Michael sat down and ate his spongy chicken sandwich, examining the novel Mr. Mitchell had handed out at the end of class: *The Outsiders*. His eyes caught a few odd words on the back cover—*Ponyboy, cussed,* and *greaser*—but his mind kept wandering.

What would it be like to have friends to eat lunch with? he wondered.

He looked away from his book for a moment and spotted Zoe on the far side of the cafeteria, eating with another girl. Michael imagined walking over to join them. Other kids did stuff like that all the time.

But not me, Michael thought darkly as he returned to staring at his book.

"What's happenin', Speedy?"

A rough hand landed on Michael's shoulder. Startled, he recoiled to see Brandon was standing right next to him, grinning meanly.

"Must suck to have to eat alone 'cause you got no friends," Brandon taunted, looking back at friends sitting at a nearby table. "No one wants to be seen with *you*. You're so—"

"Hey, man, cut it," a deep voice boomed from the other end of the table. "He's not bothering you." The older guys glared at Brandon. The one who had nodded at Michael earlier continued speaking. "I don't know where you came from, but it ain't like that here at Bluford. Mind your business and move on."

Brandon's mouth fell open. He pointed at Michael and said, "But he can't even—"

"Man, can't you hear?" A second guy interrupted. Michael noticed he had the beginning of a beard. "Marcus told you to *move on*. I suggest you do it."

Brandon grumbled but retreated back to his friends.

Michael thanked the older guys at his table, but his face burned with shame at what had happened. He knew what Brandon said was true. He had no friends, and he hated that he needed older guys to protect him. When Michael left the cafeteria, he wished he could just disappear. For the rest of the day, he moved like a ghost through the school, sitting near the back of each room and remaining silent, never drawing any attention to himself. He imagined fading away until he disappeared completely.

After his final class, Michael lingered by his locker until most students had cleared out. Then he made his way to Ms. Spencer's office, his palms sweating. All day, he had been trying to think of what he could have done to make the principal want to contact Aunt Nora.

"Have a seat, Michael," Ms. Spencer said with her familiar warm smile as he entered her office. "How have your first two days been?"

"Um, fine," Michael replied. Ms. Spencer didn't *seem* mad at him. But why else would she want to send a note home?

"I wanted to check in with you about a few things, if that's okay." Ms. Spencer's expression turned serious, and she folded her hands on her desk.

Uh oh, Michael thought. *Here it comes.*

"I'm wondering if you could tell me what kind of guardian your aunt has been for you. Has she been treating you all right these past eight years?"

"Yeah," Michael answered uncertainly. "I guess."

"Are you getting enough to eat? Boys your age grow quickly, and sometimes it takes a while for your weight to catch up to your height. But you seem very thin. Are you hungry?"

Michael's face burned again. He *knew* he was skinny, but did Principal Spencer have to talk about it?

"I guess I'm hungry...sometimes," Michael said with a shrug. He didn't see any reason not to be honest about that. "But I like the food here in the cafeteria," he added, hoping that would make the principal happy. Ms. Spencer frowned at his answer and wrote something down.

"And how has your leg been these past two days? I wanted to remind you again that taking the bus is definitely an option. It goes right past your house and could pick you up on the corner."

Michael shook his head and looked down. "Like I told you, it's all good. I don't need to take the bus."

Ms. Spencer sighed. "Have you ever talked to anyone about being hungry or about how things are going with your aunt? Perhaps a guidance counselor at your old school?"

Michael shook his head again. He had never mentioned private details to any of his school counselors. He felt strange even now talking to Ms. Spencer.

For a moment, the principal typed at her computer. Then a printer began whirring on her desk. A second later, Ms. Spencer grabbed the letter from the machine, signed it, and placed it in an envelope with Aunt Nora's name on it.

"I don't want to leave you in the dark about this note," she confessed, taking a deep breath. "This is something that our school social worker usually handles, but she's on leave with a new baby, so I'm doing it myself. I have called a friend of mine from DHS, and someone will be coming to meet you and your aunt on Thursday. This note is to let your aunt know. If there is any problem with this, she should call me. My telephone number is in the note."

"Wait, someone's coming to our apartment? She's my aunt. W-why does DHS or whatever need to do that?" Michael stammered. He knew Aunt Nora would be furious.

"They need to check to make sure you're being taken care of," Ms. Spencer explained. "It seems as though your middle school had some management problems and was not always looking out for students. I imagine that's why DHS was never contacted. But things are different here at Bluford. I can't just ignore your situation, Michael." She paused thoughtfully. "You understand, right?"

Michael nodded, but he didn't understand at all. Except for when he was very young, no one at his school had ever asked him how he was feeling or if things were okay at home.

"It's just that...I don't think my aunt will like this," Michael confessed.

"Perhaps not," Ms. Spencer said crisply as she walked Michael out of her office. "But my concern is for you right now, not your aunt."

Michael stumbled home in a daze. He put the letter on the kitchen table where his aunt always set down her purse. Then he went to his bedroom to wait, staring numbly out his window at the gloomy, overcast sky until his aunt came home from work.

"Michael! Get over here RIGHT NOW!" Her angry shout blasted through the apartment.

When Michael limped into the tiny kitchen, Aunt Nora shook the letter in his face. "Boy, what you been telling your school about me?" she growled.

"I haven't said anything," Michael insisted.

"Then why is this woman asking questions about whether I am taking good care of you?" Aunt Nora yelled. She stepped right up to Michael and shook her finger in his face. "Now, you listen here. I took you in after your mother died. I've done everything for you! And now you've called the dogs on me. This note says that someone from DHS will be here on Thursday!"

"It's not my fault," Michael tried to explain. "Ms. Spencer is doing it, not me."

"Let me tell you what *is* gonna be your fault," Aunt Nora hissed angrily. "If you don't watch what you say when DHS is here, you're going to end up in foster care. You'll have to move *again* and live with strangers in who-knows-what part of town! Is that what you want?"

Michael swallowed hard and shook his head. He had heard bad things about foster care.

"So, this is the thanks I get for treating you like family," Aunt Nora grumbled as she slammed the letter down on the table. "Your mother never did show me any respect. Guess you're just like her. Get outta here! I don't want to see your ungrateful face no more!"

Michael fled to his room and listened to his aunt banging things around and shouting on the phone to a friend about her "spoiled nephew." But then the conversation grew quiet. After a while, Aunt Nora called him back to the kitchen. Her expression had changed—she seemed more irritated now than angry. Then she handed Michael three twenty-dollar bills.

"I want you to go down to Corner Thrift and find some new clothes for school. Bring back the change and receipt, and place them right here on the table for me."

"*Now?*" Michael was puzzled. He stared at the cash in his hands. It was the most money she had ever given him for anything.

"Yes, now!" she huffed, rereading Ms. Spencer's letter. "Go on. I got things to do."

Corner Thrift was nearly empty when Michael limped in just after seven o'clock. An old man sat behind the counter reading a newspaper and munching potato chips. He stopped and looked up as Michael moved awkwardly to a rack of shoes.

"It's almost closin' time," the man called out to Michael with a scowl.

"I'll be quick," Michael said hurriedly. "I'm just looking for some stuff for school."

"Well, good luck with that," the old man said with a short laugh. "Everything's been picked through pretty good already."

The man turned back to his newspaper, and Michael browsed around until he found a pair of scuffed Adidas that were a little big, but he figured he could stuff some socks in the toes until he grew into them. With the way he dragged his right foot, Michael wore down shoes quickly. He looked down at his feet and spotted a small hole in the side of his shoe where his white sock was visible. He wondered if Ms. Spencer had seen it earlier—or Zoe.

Next, Michael found a pair of jeans that looked slightly newer than the ones he was wearing. Finally, he picked out two plain T-shirts and a decent-looking dark gray hoodie. He was careful not to buy anything unusual that would make him stand out. But then he saw a shirt that had small dog paw prints on it. It looked just as if a dog with muddy paws had walked across the shirt. Staring at it, Michael remembered Zoe saying how much she loved stray cats and dogs.

Michael took the shirt off the hanger. It cost only $3.99, and it looked as good as new.

Probably no one would even notice it, Michael thought nervously as he turned the shirt over in his hands. *But Zoe would.*

When Michael got home, he placed the change and receipt on the table and retreated to his room. He folded the new jeans and hoodie and placed them on his chair to wear the next day. Then, feeling a little embarrassed, Michael pulled the dog print shirt out from the bottom of the bag. He stared at it briefly and then stuffed it in the very back of a dresser drawer.

Michael wasn't sure if he would ever wear the shirt, but when he thought about Zoe smiling at it, he thought that maybe—*maybe*—someday, he might.

Chapter 8

On Wednesday, Michael's routine at Bluford changed. Mr. Dooling announced that all students who had been excused from gym class would now report to study hall. Michael followed several students—a muscular boy with a cast on his arm, a girl on crutches who'd sprained her ankle during a cheer routine, and Joe Davis with his asthma—down a new corridor. The group seemed sad and quiet as they moved down the hallway, yet Michael was certain that he was the only one of them who would be there all year.

But when the small group finally reached the classroom, Michael was surprised to see a boy in a wheelchair sketching at a nearby desk. When Michael limped over to a seat near him, the boy looked up and smiled.

"What happened to your leg, man?" the boy asked matter-of-factly. Then he reached out his left fist and said, "I'm Dontay."

Michael felt confused. Why would Dontay care about his leg when *he* was in a wheelchair? Wouldn't he just want to keep quiet? Still, Michael reached out and bumped Dontay's fist.

"I'm Michael," he answered, looking around and hoping that none of the other students were listening. "I hurt my leg when I was little, and it never healed right. Sometimes it's a little hard for me to walk. No big deal."

Michael tried to act as if his leg didn't bother him, but there was something in Dontay's eyes that told Michael he wasn't convinced. The two boys sat in silence for a moment, and Michael snuck a quick glance at Dontay's legs. They seemed small and withered, but Dontay didn't seem to care. He wore brightly colored basketball shoes on each foot.

"What…what about you?" Michael asked hesitantly. He knew the question was personal, but he couldn't help it. He hoped it wouldn't make Dontay angry.

"Well, kinda like you, it happened when I was little," Dontay said, looking down at his legs. “I was in a bad car accident. It damaged my spinal cord so I couldn’t walk anymore.” Dontay paused and held up his right hand. “And it did this, too.”

Michael stared wide-eyed. Dontay’s hand was missing a thumb and index finger.

“My hand got messed up. I had to learn how to write and draw with my left hand instead. For a couple years, everything I wrote looked like chicken scratch. Not anymore, though.”

“Oh, wow,” Michael said. “That’s crazy.”

“Yeah,” Dontay agreed. “Nothing I can do about my hand, but my doctor says they’re always coming up with new treatments for spinal cord injuries. Who knows? Maybe one day I’ll walk again. We’ll see.”

Michael’s mind spun with everything Dontay said. For a second, he couldn’t speak.

“What does your doctor say?” Dontay asked, breaking the silence. “Seems like they should be able to fix an injured foot.”

Michael shrugged. “I haven’t been to a doctor about it, not in years anyway.”

“What?!” Dontay said in surprise. “Why not?”

Michael repeated what his aunt always told him—that doctors said his leg would get better on its own as he got older.

Dontay listened closely but shook his head several times.

"You seriously gotta get to the doctor," Dontay insisted. "No disrespect to your aunt, but if you're hurting, you need to get checked out."

Michael shrugged. He could barely remember a time his leg didn't hurt. Still, he couldn't imagine Aunt Nora doing anything for him, let alone taking him to a doctor—especially now. Michael looked down and noticed Dontay's drawing. It was a detailed sketch of a lion with two cubs.

"Man, that's amazing!" Michael said. The lions seemed lifelike and ready to jump from the page. "How'd you learn to do that?"

"Practice," Dontay admitted. "Lots of it. I can't play basketball or run or anything like that, so I focus on the stuff that I *can* do. You know what I mean?"

Michael nodded. Again, Dontay's words swirled in his mind and shook his insides.

"Anyway, my girlfriend is crazy about lions, so that's what I'm working on now." Dontay grabbed a pencil, as Michael's eyes widened.

"Girlfriend?" Michael exclaimed, immediately wishing he hadn't sounded so shocked. But Dontay didn't seem to mind.

"Yeah, girls really go crazy over guys in wheelchairs," Dontay said with a snort. Then he grinned in a mischievous way and added, "I don't know why I stay with her. She's always pushing me around and talking behind my back."

Michael just stared at Dontay. "What do you mean?"

"C'mon, man. Don't you get it?" Dontay asked with a sudden burst of laughter. "Pushing me around? Talking behind my back?"

"Aw, man," Michael said with a laugh and a groan. "That's bad."

"I know, right?!"

Both boys were still giggling when the teacher at the front of the classroom told everyone to quiet down and do their homework. Dontay put a textbook in front of his drawing so that the teacher couldn't see what he was doing. Then he grinned at Michael and continued sketching.

For the whole period, Michael watched the drawing come to life. And he thought about his new friend. Dontay was in a wheelchair and couldn't walk. Yet he didn't seem to want to hide or be invisible. Instead, he was friendly, outgoing, funny—even confident. And he had a girlfriend! Michael wasn't sure what to think about all that, but he knew how it made him feel. Somewhere deep inside him, hope began to flicker.

Walking home after school, Michael was so deep in thought that he didn't notice the person sitting on his front step.

"There you are!" gushed a familiar voice.

Michael nearly stumbled at the sound. He turned to see an older woman with graying hair and tired, soulful eyes beaming at him.

"Mrs. Sutton!" Michael exclaimed, his voice choking with emotion. "I can't believe it's you. How did you find me?"

"I went by your aunt's old house, and a neighbor gave me this address," Mrs. Sutton explained. She surveyed the block for a second, and Michael could see she didn't approve, but her eyes brightened when she looked at him. "It's so good to see you, Michael. It's been such a long time. You got so big and handsome!"

A flood of emotion swept over Michael. He hadn't seen her in nearly four years. For an instant, he could barely speak.

"I thought…" Michael began as tears brimmed in his eyes. "I thought I'd never see you again."

"Well, now, of course you were gonna see me again, Michael." She walked over and put her hand on his back. "I'd find you no matter where you moved! You know I love you."

Her touch cut right through all the walls Michael had built to hide his emotions. It had been years since anyone had spoken of love to him, years since he felt truly cared for.

Michael threw his arms around his old babysitter and, before he knew it, was sobbing. Mrs. Sutton didn't speak. Instead, she hugged Michael tightly and let him cry. Michael didn't care if the neighbors saw him weeping and clinging to this old woman. Embracing Mrs. Sutton was like taking in great gulps of oxygen after having been underwater for too long.

"Now, let's just you and me sit here and talk a little while," Mrs. Sutton said when Michael calmed down and wiped his eyes.

"You can come inside if you want," Michael offered.

Mrs. Sutton frowned and shook her head. "No, I don't want to go into Nora's without her knowing. Your aunt has never liked me, and I don't want to make things worse for you." Her face became very serious then, and she added, “I can see that life with your aunt has not been easy.”

Michael knew that Mrs. Sutton understood his situation better than anyone. There was no reason to hide anything.

“Sometimes things are pretty hard. I’m not gonna lie,” he admitted.

Mrs. Sutton took his hand in hers and sat quietly for a moment, watching cars pass by on the street. Then she turned toward Michael again.

“I came by today to let you know I’m moving to North Carolina to live with my daughter.” Mrs. Sutton’s eyes welled with tears as she spoke. “Henry passed away last month. Michael, I would have kept visiting you if he hadn’t been so sick. You know that, don’t you? I’ve thought of you every single day.”

Michael squeezed Mrs. Sutton’s hand tightly and nodded. He had thought of her often, too, and he was certain she knew it.

For the next couple hours, they talked as they had years ago when she babysat him after school. Michael confided to her how difficult the move had been last year and how frightening the start of high school was. He admitted that he sometimes wished he could fade away when kids stared at him. For so long, Michael had refused to share his feelings with anyone. But now, with Mrs. Sutton listening, Michael found himself saying more in two hours than he had in years.

After a long pause, Mrs. Sutton examined him closely.

"How's your leg these days?" she asked. "Is it still sore all the time?"

Michael nodded. "Yeah. Most days," he admitted.

Mrs. Sutton shook her head bitterly. "You know your Mama was gonna get it fixed for you, right? She was working long hours to set aside money for a special operation for you before she passed. I thought Nora got that money and woulda used it for you by now. I guess I was wrong."

Michael had never heard this before. All his aunt ever said was that he'd outgrow the problem.

"Is she feeding you enough?" Mrs. Sutton added then, inspecting him for a second. "You look awful thin to me." She frowned and mumbled mostly to herself, "That woman was always so resentful of your mother. I *knew* she was too selfish to take good care of you!"

Mrs. Sutton opened her big purse and pulled out a round tin container. "I made you some of your favorite cookies from back in the day," she said with a grin. "Lord, if I'd known how skinny you were, I would have brought more!"

"Yes!" Michael cheered, quickly opening the tin. "These are the *best!*"

He bit into a buttery chocolate chip cookie and closed his eyes. It was almost as if he was six again, warm and safe in Mrs. Sutton's apartment, waiting for Mom to walk through the door and put her arms around him. Suddenly, he found it hard to swallow around the lump in his throat.

"I still miss Mom so much," he blurted out.

"Oh, baby, of course you do!" Mrs. Sutton said as she put her arm around Michael's shoulders. "I miss her too. She was one of my dearest friends."

Mrs. Sutton pulled out a tissue and patted her eyes.

"Life has hurt you badly, Michael," Mrs. Sutton said firmly. "Your mother was your world, and suddenly she was gone. That's some of the worst kind of pain, and it will always be with you. But let me tell you what your mother would want you to do. She would want you to heal yourself and not just be a victim. She would want you to have faith in yourself. She would want you to build a good life. You must do that for yourself and for your mother. Do you understand what I'm telling you?"

Michael was silent for a moment. Then, slowly, he nodded his head.

"I think I do," he said. "But it's hard to do all alone."

"You don't *have* to do it all alone, Michael." Mrs. Sutton put her hands on Michael's shoulders and turned him to face her. "There are good people out there who will help—if you show you're willing to be helped. Don't underestimate the goodness of people. You gotta take the first step, Michael, and know that you are worthy of it—"

"What's going on here?" Aunt Nora's harsh voice cut through their conversation as she approached from the sidewalk.

"Oh, hello, Nora," Mrs. Sutton said tersely. "Me and Michael are just having us a talk."

"I don't recall asking you to come over," Aunt Nora grunted as she pushed past Mrs. Sutton and went up the steps to the apartment entrance. She went inside and slammed the door behind her. Mrs. Sutton sighed and shook her head.

"I swear, that woman could not be *less* like her dear sister," she muttered, smoothing out her dress. Michael noticed tears in her eyes. "Well, Michael, I'd better say goodbye. I don't think I'll be able to come see you again, but I promise you I'm gonna stay in touch. Maybe someday when you're a grown man, you'll come visit me in North Carolina." She took out a piece of paper and jotted down her new address.

"I will," Michael said with a big nod as he pocketed the paper. "You can count on that."

Mrs. Sutton hugged Michael tightly one last time and then touched his face gently. "Always remember, Michael—you're gonna heal from all this hurt. I have faith in you."

Michael watched as Mrs. Sutton slowly walked toward the bus stop, disappearing into the late afternoon flow of people. Then he sat back down on the step and replayed the visit, thinking about everything Mrs. Sutton had said. By the time he went back inside, the sun had set.

"What'd *she* want?" Aunt Nora snapped angrily as she put a plastic container in the microwave.

"She's moving to North Carolina," Michael said carefully. "She just came by to say goodbye. That's all."

Aunt Nora waited at the microwave, shaking her head. "That woman never could mind her own business. Good riddance." Then she pulled out the container and plopped it on the table.

"I brought this home for you from the cafeteria at work, so don't be saying I never do nothing for you." She pointed at a mix of green beans, chicken, and rice. "Tomorrow, you'd better watch what you say to that DHS person. You say the wrong things, and you're gonna end up in some foster home wishing you'd kept your mouth shut."

Aunt Nora stormed out of the kitchen, leaving Michael alone with his bowl of half-warmed food. The fury he felt toward his aunt for what she had hidden from him all these years made everything taste bitter. He tossed aside her food and grabbed the cookies from Mrs. Sutton's tin.

I have faith in you...

Each cookie was heavenly—filled with Mrs. Sutton's compassion and love. Michael thought about her words and the people he had already met at Bluford High: Cooper and Tarah, Ms. Spencer, Zoe, Mr. Mitchell, and now Dontay. They had all been kind to him.

"Don't underestimate the goodness of people," Mrs. Sutton had said. *"You gotta take the first step, Michael..."*

Maybe she was right, he thought. He wanted her to be, but he wasn't sure.

He closed his eyes and pictured his mother's face.

Your mother would want you to have faith in yourself.

"I'm trying, Mom," he whispered, alone in the empty kitchen, unsure what to do next.

"I'm trying."

Chapter 9

"How about you, Michael? Do you have anything to add?"

Michael looked up to see Mr. Mitchell staring at him from the front of the room. Michael was worrying so much about the visit from DHS that he had been unable to focus on the class discussion on the first chapter of *The Outsiders*.

Michael shook his head in embarrassment. Mr. Mitchell seemed surprised and almost disappointed. Michael had been quiet in his other classes, hoping no one would notice him. But until now, English class had been different. He had managed to talk in class and participate in discussions. Being involved actually made him feel good, especially with Zoe nearby.

But today, Michael didn't feel like talking to anyone. Too much was on his mind. What if he said the wrong thing to the DHS person? Would he get sent to a foster home? Michael spent the entire school day in a fog of stress. On his walk home, he barely noticed the young boys shouting insults as he passed by.

Michael was surprised to find his aunt already home and sitting in the living room when he arrived. She got up the second he walked through the door and shoved a bag into his hands.

"Go get cleaned up," she barked. "Then change into these new clothes. We ain't got much time until that DHS fool gets here."

Michael peered into the bag and was astonished to see brand new clothes—bright Nike sneakers and a crisp new shirt and jeans. Aunt Nora had never bought him anything like this before. He looked at her in surprise.

"That's right," Aunt Nora said sharply. "Now you can't say I never got you good clothes."

Michael turned away, and his aunt's angry voice followed him.

"You better watch yourself. Like I said, you say the wrong things and you gonna end up in a foster home with nasty people. Likely make you sleep in a basement and treat you worse than they would their own dog."

With trembling hands, Michael changed into the new clothes. He had barely finished buttoning up his shirt when he heard the doorbell. He wiped a film of sweat off his forehead and grabbed Mom's beach stone, placing it in his pocket.

"Michael, we have a visitor waiting to meet you!" Aunt Nora called. Her voice was so sugary sweet that it made Michael cringe.

Liar, he thought to himself as he emerged from his room. The anger he felt from the night before flared and burned in him.

"Hello, Michael. I'm Trey Robinson."

Michael reached out and shook the outstretched hand of the chubby, middle-aged Black man who now stood in their living room. Mr. Robinson's kind eyes were magnified by oversized glasses, and he focused them directly on Michael. He was surprised to see that Mr. Robinson seemed a bit nervous too.

"Why don't we all just sit down," Aunt Nora suggested in a singsong voice. "Michael, you sit over there in your favorite place."

Aunt Nora and Mr. Robinson sat down on chairs across from Michael, and he sat on the faded leather couch. It was far from his “favorite place.” In fact, in the years he had lived with his aunt, this was one of the few times he had ever been allowed to sit on it.

“Well, as you know, Principal Spencer was in touch with me,” Mr. Robinson began, pulling a clipboard and some papers out of his briefcase. “She just wanted me to see how everything has been going with you and Michael.”

“Everything’s always been fine,” Aunt Nora said quickly.

Mr. Robinson glanced over at Michael and raised his eyebrows questioningly. Michael remained silent.

“I see that DHS has been sending you support money for eight years, but you’ve never applied to adopt your nephew,” Mr. Robinson said, looking up at Aunt Nora. “That’s rather unusual.”

Aunt Nora’s forced smile faded. Michael could tell the question annoyed her. She began tapping her foot and then folded her arms.

“I never said I wanted to adopt Michael,” she explained, her voice strained like an off-key note. “I already raised one boy of my own, and I don’t need another. But I’ve been good to Michael all these years. It ain't always easy, but I've done the best I could."

Michael felt a sudden urge to shake his head, but instead he remained still.

Mr. Robinson studied Aunt Nora for a long moment and then continued. "One thing we needed to check on is why you never took Michael to a doctor for the problem with his leg."

Aunt Nora shifted uncomfortably in her chair. A dark cloud seemed to pass over her face, and the last traces of fake kindness disappeared.

"Now look here," she grumbled. "Don't be making it sound like I've done something wrong. Michael's never complained about his leg—*ever!* I never assumed I was supposed to be taking some sort of special care of him."

Mr. Robinson adjusted his glasses and leaned forward.

"Well, the state is sending you a fair amount of support money every month," he said bluntly. "It is to be used for Michael's care, including any medical expenses."

Aunt Nora sighed loudly, shook her head, and then turned to stare out the window.

Mr. Robinson shifted his attention to Michael. "Your aunt says you've never complained, but does your leg ever hurt? I noticed your limp, and, honestly, it looks as though it may be painful for you to walk."

Michael felt the old familiar humiliation rush through him, but then a new feeling bubbled up. Here was someone who was honestly trying to help him.

There are good people out there who will help you if you show you're willing to be helped. Mrs. Sutton's words echoed in Michael's mind. He raised his head and looked Mr. Robinson in the eye.

"Yes, it does hurt sometimes," Michael admitted. "Not if I just walk across the room. But if I do too much or have to walk too far, it can ache a lot."

"He's never said that!" Aunt Nora shouted. She stood up and pointed her finger at Michael. "You're just being ungrateful, as usual. I didn't have to take you in. Shoulda let you just go to a foster home, and then you'd see how good you have it!"

Mr. Robinson cleared his throat and made a few notes on his clipboard. Then he rubbed a hand on his forehead as though he had a headache.

"Michael, I need to ask you a few simple questions now. Answer them as honestly as you can. I don't want you to worry about what you *should* or *shouldn't* say. Just tell me the truth, okay?"

Michael nodded.

"What are your dinners like? Does your aunt make anything special that you like?"

Michael shook his head. He explained how she kept a few things in the cabinet for him to heat up or in the freezer for him to microwave. Sometimes she brought home takeout or extra food from the nursing home cafeteria that she managed. Mr. Robinson raised his eyebrows a few times as he spoke.

"We don't usually eat together," Michael added. "I eat by myself, clean up the kitchen, and go to my room. That's about it."

"No way I can be expected to cook meals all the time after working all day," Nora complained. "I taught the boy how to take care of himself. He's independent. He don't need me to cook for him."

Mr. Robinson wrote something on his clipboard.

"Do the two of you spend any time together?" he asked. "What do you do when you're both home?"

Michael felt awkward and a little embarrassed. He didn't want to admit that his aunt never wanted to spend time with him.

"We each do our own thing," he said, unwilling to admit the full truth. "Aunt Nora is usually watching TV or on her phone or whatever. On weekends, I go to the library or something until it starts getting late and it's okay for me to come home."

"Okay for him to come home?" Mr. Robinson repeated, his voice rising. "What does that mean?"

A new look flashed in Aunt Nora's eyes. Instead of anger, it was one of hesitation and fear. Michael had never seen it before.

"Now, you gotta understand, Mr. Robinson, as an adult, I need my time! I spend all week working in a nursing home. On the weekend, I need to rest." Aunt Nora spoke quickly and almost sounded desperate. "It ain't all like Michael says. He *wants* to go to the library. I got him a library card years ago because I knew how much he likes books."

Rage suddenly boiled in Michael's throat. It had been Mrs. Sutton who had gotten that card for him when he was eight, not Aunt Nora! He could not hold back his fury.

"You did *not*," Michael snapped, his voice slicing the air. "Don't you say that."

Aunt Nora twisted around to look at Michael. Her jaw hung open in shock. Never before had Michael spoken out against his aunt or even disagreed with her.

Michael met his aunt's angry glare for a moment, but then looked down in fear as he had done so many times before.

Mr. Robinson finally broke the silence between them. "Let me take a look at your room, Michael," he suggested, gesturing for him to come forward. "I'd like to get an idea of what your everyday living is like."

"Yeah, you go ahead and take a look," Aunt Nora grumbled. "I don't care what he tells you. I treat him right. I've done everything I ever could for him."

Mr. Robinson said nothing as he followed Michael down the cramped hall. At one point, he pointed to a smoke detector in the ceiling. "Sounds as if it needs a new battery," Mr. Robinson said with a chuckle. "Doesn't that chirping bother you?"

Michael looked at the smoke detector and barely noticed it beeping. "To be honest, it's been like that so long, I don't even hear it anymore," he admitted. Mr. Robinson sighed.

When they reached his bedroom, Michael noticed Mr. Robinson's face cloud over. Long ago, when he shared a room with Trevon, the bedroom had been decorated with posters of athletes and rappers and exotic cars. Trevon especially loved Bugattis. Their room had a shelf full of his cousin's old basketball trophies, and speakers had been mounted to the walls. Trevon even had an old recliner where he did homework and played games on his phone. But Trevon took almost everything when he left, and when they moved, Aunt Nora got rid of what remained. Now all Michael had was a small folding chair and a wobbly thrift store table where he did his homework.

The only objects that stood out were the beach stones on his windowsill, a stack of library books on the floor, and an old picture of Michael and his mother taped on the wall by the bed.

"Okay if I sit down in the chair?" Mr. Robinson asked. Michael nodded and sat across from him on the bed.

Mr. Robinson glanced at the department store bags and empty shoebox still on the floor from earlier. "Did your aunt, by any chance, buy you some new clothes for my visit?"

"Yeah. I just got some stuff at the thrift store too, so I don't really need these," Michael said, pointing at his new shoes.

"My limp wears holes in my shoes. Aunt Nora says there's no use getting good ones, but she did today."

Michael pointed to his old shoes next to the bed. The hole on the right shoe was visible.

Mr. Robinson studied it for a second. "How long did you have to wear it like this?"

"I don't know," Michael replied with a shrug. "A few months maybe."

Mr. Robinson muttered something Michael couldn't hear. Then he quickly changed subjects. "I'm wondering if you could tell me how you spend your free time. I'm guessing from that pile of books that you enjoy reading a lot."

"Yeah, definitely," Michael said, now relaxing a bit. "I don't get bored much since, you know, I can get all the books I want in the library. When I was little, I was obsessed with *Magic Tree House* 'cause there are like a hundred of them, and each one takes you away. Then I got into all the *Percy Jackson* books and then I binged on *Hunger Games.* Now sometimes I check out sci-fi or even a scary Stephen King book once in a while. They keep me awake, but they make me forget at the same time. I skip realistic books 'cause I just need to forget, you know? When I'm into a book, it feels like I'm somewhere else—instead of here. Know what I mean?"

Michael felt embarrassed to have revealed so much all at once, but Mr. Robinson was smiling and nodding enthusiastically. "I know *exactly* what you mean. I love reading too. Comic books were my jam back in the day, especially Spider-Man. My son loves the Miles Morales ones," he confessed. Then he flipped through his notes for a second, and his expression became more serious.

"I've got the name of a special doctor, called an orthopedist, who you can visit about your leg. I'll make an appointment for you to see her soon. And while we're in here, just the two of us, I need to ask you straight up: Do you want to stay with your aunt?"

Michael was startled, both by the idea of seeing a doctor, but even more by Mr. Robinson's question. He had no idea how to respond.

"I…I'm not sure," Michael began slowly. "Aunt Nora told me how I would be treated in a foster home. Sometimes… things aren't easy here, but at least I have food and a room of my own. I don't want to end up in someone's basement and get treated worse than a dog."

Mr. Robinson frowned and laughed at the same time.

"I can understand your worries, Michael. But horror stories about foster homes are the exception, not the rule. Most foster parents are wonderful people who love the kids they take in. I know this because I work with them every day. Now, I can't guarantee that you'd get placed with a family in this area. You would maybe need to switch schools, but I promise you: I would make sure you got placed with a good family. You have my word on that."

Michael rubbed his neck anxiously and looked away from Mr. Robinson. Would being a foster kid make him stand out more? Would he be even more alone? Did he really want to start all over again at another school? For some reason, Zoe and Dontay's faces flashed in his mind.

As if sensing Michael's worries, Mr. Robinson added, "Just so you know, there are hundreds of foster kids in this city. And there are support groups where you can meet other kids your age who live with foster families."

"Hundreds?!" Michael said in surprise.

"Yes," Mr. Robinson assured him. "You would definitely not be alone as a foster kid. But there is no pressure here. This all happens on your terms."

"What do you mean?"

Mr. Robinson adjusted his big glasses and leaned forward in his seat, his voice low and serious again.

"You get to decide where you want to live, Michael. Take some time to really think about it. My own impression is you can have a better life than you've had so far. You have the power to change it, if that's what you want. You understand?"

Michael nodded, his mind spinning at what he had just learned.

Aunt Nora was sitting stiffly on the edge of the couch when Michael and Mr. Robinson returned to the living room. She watched them with narrowed eyes, her jaw set rigidly.

"DHS will set up an appointment for Michael to see an orthopedist next week," Mr. Robinson announced, putting his papers in his briefcase. "I'll be in touch with you about the day and time."

"Ain't nothing some fancy doctor gonna be able to do for him. Waste of time and money," Aunt Nora huffed.

Michael saw Mr. Robinson's face stiffen with annoyance. "I think we'll let the doctors decide that, not you," he said sharply. "Here's my card. You'll hear from me next week."

He gave Michael a card too and placed a hand on his shoulder. "It was good to meet you, young man. Remember what we talked about."

Aunt Nora flew into a rage the moment Mr. Robinson closed the door.

"You're asking for it now!" she fumed, her voice scratchy and grating. "They're gonna throw you in a nasty foster home. You'll see. You wanted this to happen? Now you're gonna get it," she yelled, eyeing him as if daring him to say something.

Michael shrugged. "Whatever," he replied.

She erupted again, yelling curses as he turned his back on her. "Don't you walk away from me," she screamed.

But he did. And as he shut the door of his bedroom, Michael could feel something inside of him growing stronger and breaking free.

Chapter 10

"I'm wondering if…if I could see Principal Spencer."

Michael nervously gripped the counter in the main office early Friday morning. Secretary Bader picked up her phone and spoke briefly to Ms. Spencer, and then nodded.

"Go right in," Ms. Bader said.

Michael had decided late last night to speak to Ms. Spencer before classes started. *It's not a big deal*, Michael told himself, trying to calm his nerves. *But it's a first step.*

"Good morning, Michael," Ms. Spencer greeted him, smiling warmly as he entered the familiar office. "Have a seat. I hope everything went well with Mr. Robinson."

Michael nodded and sat down, taking a deep breath to collect his thoughts.

"Did you want to speak to me about his visit, or about something else?" she asked.

"Well, it's sort of about his visit," Michael began. "Some of the things Mr. Robinson said really got me thinking about…well, about me. And what I need to do."

Ms. Spencer nodded as if she agreed with what he was saying, even before he had said it.

"The truth is, it *does* hurt my leg to walk all the way to Bluford," Michael admitted, surprised at how relieved he felt saying the words to her. "Mr. Robinson is going to set up a time for me to see a doctor."

"I'm so pleased to hear it, Michael. That should have happened a long time ago," Ms. Spencer assured him. "There's no reason you should be in pain all this time. And don't worry, if you need to miss school for the appointment, that won't be a problem."

"Okay, thanks, but there is something else too," Michael continued. "I've been thinking…well, I decided it makes sense for me to ride the bus after all. Is that still something I could do?"

"Definitely!" Ms. Spencer beamed. "I'm so glad you've changed your mind. You can ride the bus home this afternoon. I'll have Ms. Bader let the driver of Bus 17 know."

Michael wanted to say something else to her too. Riding the bus meant he had to face Brandon Miller every day. He was sure

Brandon would make bus rides more painful than any walk. Yet Michael couldn't bring himself to tell Ms. Spencer, not now anyway. Instead, he decided that he would deal with Brandon on his own. The thought had kept him up last night and filled him with dread as he left the principal's office, but there was no other way forward. Standing up to Brandon was terrifying, but doing nothing to stop him was even worse.

Throughout the morning, Michael kept picturing what might happen on his bus ride home. *How many people will laugh at me?* he wondered. *How far will Brandon push things? Are we gonna fight?*

It didn't help that Mr. Mitchell's lesson focused on the first chapter of *The Outsiders*. Brandon seemed to look back at him when the class discussed how the author, a high school student, described the world as a cruel place in which power and privilege were not shared equally.

"Does privilege exist today like it does in chapter one? Does it make some of us outsiders?"

"All the time. I mean, it's different, but it definitely exists here," Michael had said, thinking about the bus ride that awaited him. "Some people just don't know how good they have it, you know? Instead, they attack others for being different. How can that be fair, when we don't get to choose what we are or how we were born? It's not fair. It's privilege."

Mr. Mitchell nodded and asked for more details. Brandon had smirked when Michael spoke up, but Michael was glad that Zoe and others seemed to agree with what he said. Zoe even praised him.

"That was awesome, Michael," she gushed at the end of class, touching his arm for an instant. He thanked her, but he could not shake his worries about what the end of the day would bring.

At lunchtime, Michael was heading to his empty table in the corner of the cafeteria when someone tapped him on the shoulder. He turned around to see a tall girl with curly black hair looking at him expectantly.

"You're Michael, right?"

He nodded.

"I'm Aliyah," she said with a smile and then pointed over to a table near the front. Michael saw Dontay waving at him. "Dontay asked me to see if you want to sit with us."

"Sure," Michael said, shocked at the offer. He wondered if Aliyah was the girl Dontay had been drawing the picture for. "Thanks."

When Michael limped over, he noticed that Dontay's table was unusual. Unlike other tables, it was designed for wheelchairs on one side and regular seats on the other. A cafeteria worker walked out of the kitchen with a tray of food and placed it in front of Dontay. Michael thought that might make him feel embarrassed, but Dontay thanked the aide and kept talking without even taking a breath.

"Hey, Michael!" Dontay said. "I saw you sitting alone yesterday. There's no reason for that." Dontay then introduced him to his friends as Aliyah pulled up a chair.

"Are you the one that likes lions?" Michael blurted out. Everyone laughed, and Aliyah's coppery complexion turned a little pink.

The conversation quickly turned to classes, the best food in the cafeteria, and riding the bus. Michael learned that Dontay took a modified bus that lifted his wheelchair inside.

"Nothing like sitting up in a floating wheelchair on Tanner Street to bring out the gawkers," Dontay joked, rolling his eyes. "One time, this guy was so busy staring at me that he walked right into a telephone pole. I was like, 'Bro, you better watch out or you're gonna end up in a chair too!'"

Careful not to stare, Michael noticed how hard Dontay had to work to eat his hamburger. Because of his missing right fingers, he used his left hand to grip the burger and the side of his right hand to balance it out. At one point, a pickle fell out on the table, but Dontay ignored it.

Watching him, Michael felt a sudden wave of shame. After all, he could walk through the cafeteria with a tray, sit at a regular table, and eat with no problem. Sure, he had a limp, but he could ride the same bus all the kids rode. And yet Michael had spent so much time focusing on what he *couldn't* do instead of—like Dontay—focusing on what was possible.

No more, Michael thought to himself as the lunch period ended. *I can do better than this.*

After his last class, Michael moved nervously through the noisy throng of students leaving Bluford High School. It took him several minutes to find his bus, and just as he reached it, he heard someone call his name. He turned to see Zoe hurrying over to him.

"I gotta get onto my bus, but I wanted to see if you'd like to watch *The Outsiders* sometime. Mr. Mitchell said there's a movie version of it. I thought it'd be cool to watch it together."

Michael nearly fell over. No girl had ever asked to spend time with him, and he had never imagined that would change. Until now, his limp and his Aunt Nora had made him an outsider. But suddenly, the world had shifted. For a split second, he wondered what to say. Then he pictured Dontay in his mind telling him to say yes. The image almost made him laugh.

"Uh…that sounds cool," Michael said shyly. Then he gathered up his courage, looked right at Zoe, and tried again. "I mean, yes. Let's watch it."

"Great!" Zoe said with a wide grin. She told him how to contact her, and then she disappeared into the crowd of students hurrying to go home.

Michael stood in a haze, watching her leave.

"Wow!" he said out loud, stunned at what just happened. But then Michael spotted Brandon getting on the bus.

For a second, he considered changing his mind and walking home, but something inside pushed him forward. Nervously, Michael joined the line. When it was his turn to board, he gripped the sidebars and pulled himself up the steps. The driver, an older woman Mrs. Sutton's age, frowned at him.

"Who are you? You on the wrong bus or something?"

"No, I'm Michael Tatem. This is my first time riding."

"Oh, that's right," the driver said, glancing at her clipboard. "They said there'd be a new stop. Well, welcome aboard, Michael. Find yourself a seat."

Michael stepped into the crowded aisle and discovered the bus was nearly packed. As he searched for an empty seat, he spotted Brandon gawking at him.

"Well, look who's here!" Brandon hollered, pointing at him. "What's up, Speedy! You finally figure out that the bus is better than limping home?"

A few kids near Brandon turned to look at Michael, but others shook their heads at him.

"Seriously, Brandon? You got problems," one boy said.

"That ain't right," someone else added.

Brandon ignored the comments and sneered at Michael.

"You got something to say, Speedy?" he taunted.

Something deep in Michael's soul flared. He was tired of pretending as though the names didn't bother him. What's more, he was angry.

"Damn right, I got something to say," Michael growled.

A sudden hush filled the bus. "Oh snap!" someone said. A few others giggled nervously. The sneer on Brandon's face vanished, and he suddenly looked surprised and confused. He clearly had not expected Michael to speak up.

"Yeah, my leg is messed up. Yeah, I have a limp. So what?" Michael fumed. "Why point out the obvious every time you see me? That's weak, if you ask me."

Brandon bolted from his seat and rushed toward Michael.

Suddenly the bus driver began shouting, "Get back to your seat! There's a camera filming you right now. If you get into a fight, you're gonna get suspended. Test me and see what happens."

Brandon stopped in his tracks and punched his fist into the back of a seat before sitting down. Michael grabbed a seat next to someone in the second row and tried to look calm, but he could feel the blood pounding in his head. His mouth had turned completely dry. The fact that he had stood up to Brandon both startled and amazed him.

Maybe that's it, Michael hoped. *Maybe that's the last time Brandon bothers me.*

But when the bus stopped at the corner near Michael's building, Brandon jumped up too.

"Come on now," the driver said in irritation to Brandon. "You know this isn't your stop."

"It is today," Brandon growled.

The driver shook her head and shut the door behind them. Michael saw students scrambling to the windows. Some pointed phones at them, trying to film what was about to happen. Michael braced for Brandon to strike him as the bus rumbled down the street and turned the corner.

"It's time, Speedy," Brandon said as he clenched his fists. "You're not gonna walk at all when I'm done."

Michael felt strangely calm. He was tired of hiding and being scared.

"I don't know what you get out of this," he said, looking Brandon in the eye. "But if you gotta hit me to feel better, go ahead. It's not like I can run away."

Brandon glanced to either side of the street as if he thought someone was watching. "You just want me to punch you so you can go crying to your mommy and get me in trouble."

Michael shook his head. "Nah, man. My mom died when I was six. Nothing you can do to me will hurt worse than that."

For a second, Michael thought he saw a flash of confusion in Brandon's eyes, and maybe even a glimmer of guilt. But just as quickly, Brandon tried to act tough again.

"You're lying. You're just trying to make me feel sorry for you. That don't work with me," Brandon said.

"I wish I were lyin', bro. You wanna come to the cemetery with me and see for yourself?" Michael asked, the last of his fear draining away.

Brandon's eyes widened. Michael watched him look up and down the empty street again. The air grew strangely still and quiet.

"Forget you, Speedy," he said finally. "I'm outta here."

Michael remained motionless as Brandon stormed away. At the end of the block, Brandon turned back one last time and quickly disappeared around the corner. In that moment, Michael knew Brandon would not bother him again.

"I need to know if you're staying or leaving." Aunt Nora spoke from the doorway of his room later that night. Her voice seemed wearier than usual. When he didn't answer right away, she threw her hands up in the air. "If you're stupid enough to leave family and live with total strangers, I can't help you."

Michael toyed with Mr. Robinson's card as she continued, a note of panic creeping into her voice.

"You don't know how good you got it! Haven't I always taken care of you? Look at you sitting here—you got a room to yourself. New clothes...and...you ain't ever appreciated it!"

Michael dropped the card and faced her. "I don't mean nothing to you, remember? I've got to do what's best for me. I've got to take care of myself now," he said.

Aunt Nora muttered something under her breath that Michael couldn't hear. "Well, I brought dinner home for you from work again," she said angrily as she turned to leave. "Can't say I never did anything for you. Ungrateful and spoiled is what you are! Just like your mother—"

"You kept her money, didn't you?" he asked then, cutting her off.

"What?"

"The money my mom saved for my operation. You *stole* it. Admit it."

"How do you even..." her voice trailed off. "That was a long time ago, and I—"

"Don't talk about my mother no more," Michael said then. He limped to the door and shut it on her.

For a long time, Michael leaned back in his chair and gazed out the window at the sunset. Bittersweet feelings bubbled up in him. There was disappointment and sadness, knowing that Aunt Nora would never change. There had been a time years ago when he hoped she might actually care for him. He now realized that would never happen.

At the same time, he felt a new and unfamiliar sweetness flowing within him. There was a sense of hope in his life that he hadn't experienced in years. Unlike his aunt, Michael knew he *would* change. And he knew that, when the time to move on arrived, he would be ready.

That night, before going to bed, Michael reached back in his dresser drawer and pulled out the T-shirt with the dog paw prints on it. Thinking about wearing it for Zoe gave him a funny, jittery feeling in his stomach. He picked up the smooth beach stone, hoping for the sense of peace it often gave him. Before long, he drifted off….

Then Michael was standing on the beach, feeling a warm breeze on his face and listening to the waves crashing gently on the shore. Suddenly, he saw a woman waving to him. As she grew closer, Michael realized it was his mother.

"Mom!" he shouted joyfully. And then he was walking toward her with no pain and no limp. It felt like the most natural thing in the world. It was as though he had always been able to walk normally but hadn't figured out how until that very moment. Then he and Mom were together, laughing and hugging.

Mom grabbed his hands and felt the black stone in them.

"I love you, Michael," she said, smiling gently. "I love you," she repeated, her voice sounding like the waves and the wind and music in the air.

When Michael awoke in the morning, the stone was still in his hand, its warmth flowing through him. He lay there thinking about the day and the weeks to come. He knew that challenges awaited, but that whatever happened, he would find a way to keep moving forward.

And somehow, after everything, he felt less alone.

Want to know the full story about Darcy, Tarah, Hakeem, and Cooper? Read these Bluford Series books!

Jamee and Darcy are sisters, but they're not alike.

Check out these books about Jamee and her friends to see another, edgier side of Bluford High.

Think boys have it easy at Bluford High? Guess again.

See their struggles in these gripping titles.

Ever imagine what it's like to transfer to Bluford High, with the weight of the world on your shoulders?

Martin Luna will tell you—in his own words.

The TP Bluford Series

Stories to Experience

. . . and more titles coming soon!